Brain Juice

Look out for more books in the Goosebumps Series 2000
by R.L. Stine:

Brain Juice

R.L. Stine

Hippo

Scholastic Children's Books
Commonwealth House, 1–19 New Oxford Street, London WC1A 1NU, UK
a division of Scholastic Ltd
London ~ New York ~ Toronto ~ Sydney ~ Auckland
Mexico City ~ New Delhi ~ Hong Kong

First published in the USA by Scholastic Inc., 1998
First published in the UK by Scholastic Ltd, 1999

ISBN 0 439 01115 9

Typeset by Rowland Phototypesetting Ltd, Bury St Edmunds, Suffolk
Printed by Mackays of Chatham plc, Chatham, Kent.

10 9 8 7 6 5 4 3 2 1

Prologue

"We are wasting our time here, Morggul," the taller alien whispered. His lower mouth turned down in a tight frown as his upper mouth spoke the words.

"Gobbul, you are always so impatient," his partner scolded.

The two aliens were green and wet-skinned. They wore no clothing. Their bell-shaped bodies had four slender tentacles poking out of the sides. Two flat, webbed feet—eight curled black toes on each foot—rested at the end of short, stumpy legs.

Froglike heads bobbed on top of the short, fat bodies. The aliens' faces were ugly and cruel. Two wet yellow eyes bulged over two jagged-toothed mouths.

Purple pods throbbed and pulsed up and down their four coiling tentacles. The pods looked like deep wounds. They opened and closed, making a soft sucking sound, as the aliens breathed through them.

1

Gobbul, the taller one and the leader, had silvery tusks, much like walrus tusks, that curled over his two mouths. Morggul was fatter and slow-moving. His four tentacles were always twisting slowly through the air as if he were swimming.

The two aliens had been hiding in the home of Dr Frank King, in Maplewood, New Jersey, for nearly a week. When they weren't spying on the famous scientist, Morggul slept, snoring through both mouths. And Gobbul worried.

"We cannot spend any more time on this planet," Gobbul whispered to his partner. "Someone will find our spaceship. The humans will drag it away to study it. And we will be stranded in this horrible place for ever."

"It's well hidden in thick woods," Morggul reminded him.

"I don't want to be stranded here!" the taller one exclaimed, licking his tusks with both tongues, as he always did when he became excited. "Can you *imagine* having to live in a place where they kill their food *before* eating it?!"

"We know they were primitive people," Morggul replied. "We knew they were not very clever."

"Yes, yes. I know. That's why we've come here." Gobbul groaned. "The humans should make excellent slaves. But so far, it doesn't look promising."

2

All of Morggul's pods opened at once as he yawned. The breath that burst from his body shook the boxes and jars in the little pantry behind the kitchen where they were hiding.

"Shhh. Cover your pods when you yawn," Gobbul scolded. "We don't want Dr Frank King to discover us—do we?"

Morggul sniggered. His fat, shiny, wet body jiggled as he laughed. He narrowed his two yellow eyes. "I'm not afraid of the human. If he spots me, I'll jam one tentacle into his chest, pull out his heart, and eat it."

Gobbul frowned with both mouths. "Don't make me hungry."

"Are you sure we are in the right house?" Morggul demanded.

"Yes," Gobbul answered without hesitating. "He is the smartest of all humans. You read the sign above his front door: *DR FRANK KING, EXPERIMENTAL SCIENCE LABS*. You saw his name. King. Dr Frank *King*. That means he is the *king* of all the scientists!"

"I know," Morggul groaned, bouncing up and down on his stumpy legs. "That's why we're watching him. Because he is the king of the scientists. But he and his wife don't seem that bright to me. And they are not young enough."

"We may have to use the Brain Energizer Fluid," his leader whispered. "We must bring two human slaves back to our homeland. And

3

they've got to be young and strong and clever—clever enough to be good slaves."

"But where will we find them?" Morggul wondered.

Gobbul opened his mouths to speak—but stopped at the ring of the doorbell.

"Shhh. Dr King has visitors, Morggul. Quick—back in the cupboard. Hide."

Nathan Nichols pressed the doorbell and took a step back off the doormat. He heard the ring inside his uncle's house.

Nathan turned to his stepsister Lindy. "Are you sure we're doing the right thing?"

Lindy twisted a strand of her long, copper-coloured hair. "If Uncle Frank can't help us, no one can," she murmured. She gazed up at the brass sign over the door:

DR FRANK KING
EXPERIMENTAL SCIENCE LABS

"But maybe Uncle Frank will just think we're stupid," Nathan groaned.

"Well . . . so does everyone else," Lindy sighed.

"But what can he do for us?" Nathan demanded. "You and I . . . we'll never be clever kids."

"Uncle Frank is the cleverest person we know," Lindy replied, tangling and untangling the strand of hair around her finger. "He'll help us. I know he will."

They heard footsteps approaching inside the house.

Lindy let go of her hair and tossed it over her shoulder. Nathan cleared his throat nervously. He shoved his hands deep into the pockets of his baggy khakis.

Nathan and Lindy were both twelve. With his dark eyes, black-rimmed eyeglasses, short, curly black hair, and solemn expression, Nathan looked older.

Lindy was tall and thin. She had long, straight auburn hair that she constantly played with, and sparkling green eyes. Her mum told her she was pretty. But Lindy complained that her nose was too flat and her face was too round.

Lindy's mum had married Nathan's dad when the kids were in Year Three. They had been as close as any real brother and sister ever since.

Too close, Lindy thought. We're *too much* alike.

Why couldn't one of us have been *clever*?

The front door finally swung open. Uncle Frank's eyes bulged with surprise and his round cheeks turned red. "Well! What a nice surprise!"

He was a big Santa Claus of a man. White hair, unbrushed, sticking out in all directions over a chubby-cheeked, smiling face.

He had broad shoulders and big hands and a big belly that bounced when he laughed.

He almost always wore white. White sweatshirts over white tracksuit trousers. White trainers. White lab coats when he was working.

"Hey, Jenny! Come and see who came to visit!" he boomed to his wife. He stepped back to allow them inside.

Nathan smelled food from the kitchen. A roast, maybe, or a chicken. "Are you still eating dinner?" he asked his uncle.

"No. Just finished. Your aunt Jen is cleaning up." He turned and called again. "Jenny? Jen?"

Placing a big hand on each kid's shoulder, he guided them into the cluttered living room. "Nathan? Lindy? What's going on?" he asked. "What brings you all the way over here?"

"Well . . ." Nathan hesitated. He glanced at his stepsister.

Lindy sighed. "It's sort of a long story," she said.

Their bad day started when Mr Tyssling, their teacher, asked them to stay after school.

"But we didn't do anything!" Lindy protested.

"I know," Mr Tyssling replied with a strange smile.

John Tyssling was a tall, lanky man who always looked as if he needed a shave. He wore jeans and sweaters torn at the neck, and a lot of kids thought he was really cool.

Nathan and Lindy liked him too. But they always seemed to be on his bad side.

Mr Tyssling made Nathan and Lindy sit in front of his desk while he thumbed through test papers. "Yes. Here," he grunted, pulling out two papers.

He scratched his dark hair and narrowed his eyes at them, peering over the tests. "You both failed the termly maths test," he announced.

Nathan swallowed hard. Lindy groaned and lowered her eyes to the rucksack at her feet.

"I can't believe you both did so badly," the teacher said, shaking his head. "I mean, you had to be *cheating* to do *this* badly! You couldn't have done it on your own!"

Nathan and Lindy didn't utter a sound.

Mr Tyssling laughed, a dry laugh. "That was a joke, guys," he said. "I was trying to keep it light. I know you didn't cheat."

"Oh," Nathan murmured softly.

Lindy played with a thick strand of her hair.

Mr Tyssling waved the test papers in front of them. "So what happened?"

"We—we're just not good at maths," Lindy blurted out.

"The test was too hard," Nathan said.

"I gave you revision sheets," Mr Tyssling said, lowering the tests to the desk. "Did you use them to revise?"

"Yes," Nathan and Lindy replied in unison.

"We revised a lot," Lindy insisted.

"It was just too hard," Nathan repeated.

The teacher gazed at Nathan, then at Lindy. "Do you need extra help?" he asked. "Did you ever talk to your parents about a maths tutor? Think that might help?"

"Maybe," Lindy muttered, twisting her hair.

"We're just not bright enough," Nathan sighed.

"What did you say?" Mr Tyssling cried. He leaned across the desk. "Nathan, don't ever say that again. Of *course* you're bright enough. Don't get down on yourself like that. You just have to work harder and revise better."

"Yeah. Okay," Nathan uttered, startled by the teacher's reaction.

A few minutes later, he and Lindy were walking home. It was a blustery winter day. A strong gust of icy wind blew Nathan's green-and-white Jets cap off, and he had to chase it across the street.

He heard kids laughing. He spun around and saw Ellen Hassler, Wardell Greene and Stan Garcia—three kids from his class—hooting and pointing.

The Clever Kids, Nathan thought bitterly.

He tugged the cap low on his head. Then he kept one hand on it as he ran back across the street to his stepsister.

Ellen, Wardell and Stan got nothing but A's. Mr Tyssling was always calling on them, always asking them to come up to the blackboard and solve problems.

The three of them always seemed to be together. Like some kind of Brains Club, Nathan thought. *Only clever kids can hang out with us!*

"Why can't we be clever too?" he muttered as the wind blew the Jets cap into the street again.

Lindy narrowed her eyes at him. "Excuse me?"

"What I said to Mr Tyssling was right," Nathan said. "We're just not clever enough. Why can't we be like those kids over there?" He pointed across the street. "They're all geniuses!"

Lindy shrugged. She zipped up her red-and-blue anorak. "I don't care about being a genius. I just don't want to fail maths!"

They opened the front door to find Brenda, Lindy's five-year-old sister, waiting for them. Brenda looked like a small version of Lindy. She had the same green eyes, pale skin, and auburn hair.

"What took you so long?" she demanded sharply, crossing her arms in front of her slender chest. She was on her knees on the carpet with colourful pieces of plastic strewn around her.

"We had to stay after school," Lindy sighed, tossing her rucksack on to an armchair.

"What are you doing down there?" Nathan demanded. "What is all that junk?"

"It isn't junk." Brenda sneered. "It's my new dolls' house. I've been waiting for Lindy to come help me put it together."

"Huh? Lindy?" Nathan felt insulted. "Why do you want Lindy to help, Brenda? Why don't you want me?"

"Because you're stupid," Brenda replied without hesitating.

"Hey!" Nathan protested angrily.

Lindy laughed.

"You can't build anything," Brenda accused, arms still crossed. She uncrossed them to tug at a strap of her denim dungarees. "Remember that model car you tried to build?"

"It had too many pieces," Nathan grumbled.

"Yes. And you glued most of them to your desk!" Lindy chimed in. She and Brenda laughed.

"I couldn't help it. There was a hole in the tube of glue!" Nathan cried.

"Well, I want Lindy to help me," Brenda declared. And then she added, "Mum said you would."

"Okay. Okay," Lindy sighed. She dropped down to the carpet beside her sister. "Let's see what we have here. Wow. There are a *million* pieces."

Nathan slid into an armchair to watch. He draped his legs over the side of the chair. "Okay, genius," he called to Lindy. "Let's see you build it."

"Shut up," Brenda told him.

"*You* shut up!" Nathan snapped back. He felt really annoyed that his little stepsister called him stupid. He thought she looked up to him.

Lindy unfolded the instruction sheet. She scanned it quickly, turning it over, glancing at the complicated drawings.

"So many pieces. . ." she murmured. "Brenda, are you sure this is just *one* dolls' house?"

"Hurry up! Build it!" Brenda insisted, impatiently punching her fists against her thighs. "Hurry!"

Lindy studied the instruction sheet. She unfolded it until it was bigger than a road map. "I . . . I don't know where to start," she cried.

"This looks like the floor," Brenda said. She handed Lindy a long, flat rectangle.

"Okay. We'll start with the floor." Lindy struggled to find it on the chart. Then she located two yellow walls. "These should fit into the floor," she murmured. "But how?"

She tried sliding the walls into narrow grooves on the ends of the floor. But they didn't fit.

Then she tried fitting in two other pieces.

"No—those are ceilings!" Brenda protested.

Nathan laughed gleefully and slapped the sides of the armchair.

"Okay, Mr Clever." Lindy groaned. "I give up. Come over here and help us."

Nathan stood up and slowly made his way across the room to them. "This looks pretty easy to me," he boasted. "No problem."

He dropped on to the carpet and took the floor piece from Lindy. The two of them struggled to find walls that fitted. Then Lindy suggested they start with the roof and work down.

But the roof came in three pieces of red plastic. And they couldn't figure out how to fit them together.

"This is a bit hard," Nathan confessed, scratching his curly black hair. He pulled off his glasses and blew a speck of dust off one lens. Then he turned back to the floor piece.

"Look. The walls have little tabs," he said. "I think if you push really hard—"

Lindy and Brenda both cried out at the sound of the *CRAAAACK*.

"You broke it! You *broke* it!" Brenda wailed.

Nathan stared down unhappily at the floor piece, cracked jaggedly in two.

"You're stupid!" Brenda shrieked, jumping to her feet. "I'm telling Mum! You're both stupid! Stupid idiots! Stupid! Stupid!"

She ran crying from the room.

Nathan let the broken floor pieces slip from his hands. He turned sadly to Lindy. "We let her down."

"I can't read these instructions," Lindy cried, holding them up again. "They're just too hard!" She furiously crumpled them up and hurled them across the room. "And we're too stupid."

"And that's why you came to see me?" Uncle Frank asked, leaning forward in his chair. His eyes moved from Nathan to Lindy. "Because you think you're stupid?"

14

"Yes," Nathan agreed, pushing his glasses up on his nose.

He and Lindy hadn't touched the brownies and milk their aunt Jenny had brought in. They both sat stiffly in chairs across from Uncle Frank, their hands clasped tightly in their laps.

"Maybe we're not really stupid," Lindy chimed in. "But we're not really clever, either."

"We're not clever *enough*," Nathan said.

Uncle Frank cleared his throat. He narrowed his eyes thoughtfully. "And what do you want me to do?"

"Well. . ." Nathan hesitated.

"You're the smartest person in our family," Lindy spoke up. "And you're a scientist, right?"

Uncle Frank nodded.

"And you do scientific work about the brain, right?" Nathan added.

Uncle Frank nodded again.

"So. . ." Nathan continued. "We thought maybe you knew some way Lindy and I could get cleverer."

"Isn't there *anything* you can do?" Lindy pleaded. "Any way at all to make us cleverer?"

Uncle Frank rubbed his chin. "Yes," he replied finally. "Yes, I do have something that might work."

"What *is* it?" Nathan and Lindy asked in unison.

15

Uncle Frank leaned forward in his chair. He started to reply—but suddenly swung around and stared at the doorway to the kitchen.

"What's wrong?" Nathan asked.

Uncle Frank turned back to them. "Did you hear something? Probably just Jenny." He shook his head. "Funny. I've had the strangest feeling that I'm being watched."

"Weird," Lindy muttered, glancing to the doorway. She didn't see anything unusual there.

Uncle Frank shrugged. "I suppose all scientists have that feeling when they're working on something top secret." He tugged down the sleeves of his white sweatshirt. He seemed to be thinking hard about something.

"So . . . do you really think you can help us?" Lindy asked eagerly.

"Yes. Yes, I do," her uncle replied after a long moment.

Nathan slapped the arms of the chair

excitedly. "You mean it? Something to make us cleverer?" he asked.

Uncle Frank nodded. "Yes. I have been working on something. But. . ." He glanced to the doorway again. "It's very top secret. And very dangerous."

Nathan gasped. Lindy swallowed hard.

"I don't know. Maybe it's too dangerous," Uncle Frank said softly.

"But—if it will work. . ." Nathan urged.

"Oh, it will work," the scientist replied. "It will definitely work. I've tested it out. I wouldn't even try it on you if I hadn't tested it out."

"So . . . can we try it?" Lindy asked.

"Can we?" Nathan cried.

Uncle Frank frowned. Once again, he seemed lost in thought.

Then he startled the kids by jumping quickly to his feet. "Okay!" he declared enthusiastically. "Okay. Okay. Let's try it."

The scientist left the kids in the living room. Humming to himself, he disappeared into his lab. A few minutes later, still humming, he made his way into the kitchen.

Jenny looked up from the kitchen table where she was writing a shopping list on a long pad. She was a pretty, blonde-haired woman, with soft brown eyes and a warm smile. "What's up, Frank? Did you and the kids finish your top secret, private talk? Can I go out and see them now?"

He motioned for her to sit still. "Poor kids," he muttered. He opened a food cupboard and began rummaging through bottles and jars.

Jenny came up beside him at the kitchen counter. "What's wrong? Why did they come to see you?"

Frank grunted as he found what he was searching for. He pulled out a small bottle of purple grape juice.

Then he turned to his wife. "Nathan and Lindy somehow got it into their heads that they're not clever."

Jenny raised her eyes from the grape juice to her husband. "Excuse me? Not clever?"

Dr King nodded. He examined the purple bottle. "The two of them are really upset. They came to ask me if I had anything to make them cleverer."

Jenny's mouth dropped open. "And what did you tell them? I hope you told them that they are both *very* bright. That they shouldn't worry about—"

He raised a finger to his lips. "I'm going to do something to build up their confidence," he whispered. "That's their whole problem. They have no confidence. They don't believe in themselves."

18

"What are you going to do?" his wife asked suspiciously.

"I think this will do the trick," the scientist replied. "I went into the lab and made a label of my own on the computer."

Dr King set the grape juice bottle on its side on the worktop. Then he held up the label he had printed:

BRAIN JUICE.

Jenny frowned at the label. "What on earth is Brain Juice?"

Dr King chuckled. "I'm going to tell them it's a secret formula that will make them smarter. You'll see. It's only grape juice, of course. But it really will help them. If they *believe* they are clever, they really will be clever."

Jenny sighed. "Worth a try, I suppose." She hurried to the living room to talk to the kids.

Dr King turned back to the bottle. He carefully stuck the *BRAIN JUICE* label over the grape juice label. Then he turned the bottle in his hand, making sure that the grape juice label didn't show through.

Perfect, he declared to himself. Perfect. You can't see the old label at all. It's now a bottle of Brain Juice.

Pleased with his clever idea, Dr King smiled to himself. Still admiring the bottle, he started to the living room with it.

The phone rang. The phone in his lab down the hall.

He set the bottle down on the worktop beside the pantry door and hurried to the lab to answer it.

As soon as the kitchen stood empty, the two aliens squeezed out of their hiding place. They bounced out of the pantry, leaving a wet stain on the floor behind them.

"Our chance, but we must hurry," Gobbul whispered, eyeing the doorway.

"Did you see those humans in the other room?" Morggul replied excitedly. "They look young and strong. If we can make them bright enough, they could be the slaves we have come for."

"Perhaps," Gobbul replied. He wrapped a green tentacle around the grape juice bottle. "We shall see. We shall see. . ."

He unscrewed the top of the bottle.

Morggul's body made a wet slapping sound on the floor as he moved closer to his leader. "If we take the children as slaves, I want to eat the scientist. And his mate. I want to eat them alive, while they're still fresh. Food tastes so much better when it's screaming."

Gobbul pushed his partner back. "Stop thinking only of your stomachs," he scolded. "We have work to do."

Morggul made a spitting sound through the purple pods up and down his arms.

Gobbul raised the Brain Juice bottle and poured the grape juice down the sink. Then he pulled another bottle of purple liquid from a pouch in his upper stomach.

Carefully, he poured his own purple liquid into the Brain Juice bottle. "Our only supply of Brain Energizer Fluid," he muttered. "Let's hope it works." He capped the bottle and placed it back on the counter.

"Hurry, Morggul." He gave his fat partner a push with all four tentacles. "Back into the pantry. Before the scientist King returns."

Morggul gazed at the purple bottle. His lower mouth frowned. His upper mouth said, "No human has ever drunk this formula. How do we know what side effects it will have? Maybe it will *kill* them!"

Gobbul gave his partner another shove. "Maybe," he replied. "We'll see. . ."

Dr King returned to the kitchen. He picked up the purple bottle and started to take it to Nathan and Lindy in the living room.

"Hey—" he muttered in surprise when his shoe slid on something on the floor. He glanced down at several small puddles.

With a groan, he bent down and wiped two fingers through it. "Sticky," he muttered. "Sort of slimy. Jenny must have spilled something."

He heard his wife and the two kids laughing about something in the other room. With another groan, he stood up and lumbered out of the kitchen.

"Here," he said, rejoining the kids. He held up the bottle. "I think this will help you two." He handed the bottle to Lindy.

She examined the label. "Brain Juice?" She narrowed her eyes suspiciously at her uncle.

Uncle Frank nodded. "My own formula. I've been working on it for many years."

Nathan took the bottle from Lindy. "This stuff will make us cleverer?" he asked. "How does it work?"

Uncle Frank dropped beside his wife on the couch. "Much too complicated to explain," he told them. "It has to do with neurons and protons. And the electrical impulses in the brain."

"It—it's going to *change* our brains?" Nathan asked, staring down at the bottle in his hand.

"No. It won't change you," Uncle Frank replied. He and Aunt Jenny exchanged glances. The kids didn't see him wink at her.

"To put it very simply, the chemicals in my Brain Juice formula knock down the roadblocks in your brain. We want to open up the highways to your memory. The Brain Juice makes the electrical impulses flow more freely."

Nathan and Lindy both gazed at the purple liquid in the bottle. "So what do we do?" Lindy asked. "How much do we drink?"

"You have to drink it all," Uncle Frank replied. "Do it tonight when you get home. Divide the liquid in half. Each of you should drink half a bottle."

"And then?" Lindy demanded.

"And then, forget about it," Uncle Frank instructed. "Don't think about it again. And don't worry about getting cleverer. Just work as hard as you can. Work harder than ever at your school-work."

23

A smile spread over his round, pink cheeks. "And then you'll see what happens. And I think you'll be very happy."

"We ... we'll be really clever?" Nathan stammered.

A horn hooted outside. Two short hoots, then a long one.

"That must be your parents," Aunt Jenny said. "They've come to pick you up." She crossed to the window and waved to them.

Uncle Frank held the Brain Juice bottle as Nathan and Lindy pulled on their coats. Then he handed it to Nathan as they made their way out the door. "Report back to me with the results," he said solemnly. "And remember, this is a top-secret experiment. Don't tell anyone."

Nathan and Lindy agreed. They thanked their uncle, then hurried to the car.

Nathan hid the bottle deep in his coat pocket. He and Lindy were dying to tell their parents about it. But top secret meant top secret.

As soon as they got home, Lindy brought two drinking glasses into Nathan's room. They carefully poured out the purple liquid, dividing it in two.

Nathan gulped. "I can't believe it," he said. The bedroom door was shut and locked, but he whispered anyway. "Do you think this stuff will really make us geniuses?"

Lindy stared down at the glass in her hand.

"Uncle Frank is a genius," she whispered. "He wouldn't lie to us."

Nathan burst out laughing. "It . . . it's going to be so *awesome!*" he cried. "I mean, *we'll* be the clever kids! Everyone in school will start thinking of *us* as the clever kids. How cool is *that?*"

"Cool," Lindy agreed.

They raised their glasses. They clinked them together the way their parents always toasted each other.

The purple liquid shimmered thickly in the glow of the desk lamp.

"I hope it tastes okay," Nathan said, hesitating.

"Just drink," Lindy instructed.

They tilted the glasses to their mouths and drank.

Nathan lowered the glass with about an inch of liquid still in it. "It's so thick," he murmured, making a face.

"Drink it all," Lindy urged. She pushed his glass back up to his face. "Drink it all, Nathan. You want to be as clever as you can, don't you?"

He held his breath and swallowed the rest.

They set the glasses down. Lindy licked some purple liquid off her lips. "Tastes a little like liquorice," she said.

"Tastes like medicine," Nathan grumbled, "Yuck." He swallowed several times, trying to get rid of the taste. "I have to get some gum or something."

"Do you feel any cleverer?" Lindy asked.

"Duhhh . . . yeah," he replied.

"Spell liquorice," she demanded.

"Huh?"

"Spell liquorice, Nathan. Go ahead."

They both knew that Nathan was the world's worst speller.

He hesitated, thinking hard. "Uh . . . l-i-k— No. L-i-c-k—"

"Stop," Lindy said, shaking her head. "The Brain Juice isn't working yet."

"It isn't supposed to be *instant!*" Nathan declared.

"I just hope it works by Wednesday." Lindy sighed.

"Huh? Why Wednesday?"

"That's the next maths test."

Nathan yawned loudly. "Wow. I suddenly feel so sleepy."

"Me too," Lindy admitted. "So sleepy I can't keep my eyes open."

Yawning, she said goodnight. Then she shuffled to her room across the hall, the strange liquorice taste lingering in her mouth.

The two aliens bobbed up the stairs, leaving puddles of dampness on the carpet behind them. By the time they reached the second floor of the

Nichols's house, they were gasping for breath, the pods on their tentacles opening and closing like fish mouths.

"It's the atmosphere on this awful planet," Gobbul whispered. "It makes us five times as heavy."

Morggul's tentacles writhed and wriggled. Waves of thick perspiration rolled off his fat body. "Maybe we shouldn't have landed in New Jersey. Maybe there are nicer places."

"Too late for that now," Gobbul replied with his upper mouth. His bottom mouth was turned down in a tight sneer.

"It took so long to get to this house," Morggul complained. "Keeping in total darkness. Hiding every time one of their vehicles rolled by. It's nearly morning, Gobbul."

"Sssshh. Do not wake anyone." Gobbul ran his tongues over his tusks. "We *had* to come to their house. We have to make sure they drank the formula."

Their bodies slapping the carpet wetly, the two aliens made their way down the dark hall. They stopped outside Nathan's bedroom and peered inside.

"The boy," Gobbul whispered. He motioned with all four tentacles for Morggul to follow him.

They stopped beside Nathan's desk. Gobbul gazed at the two empty drinking glasses on the desktop. He lowered a tentacle and sniffed the glasses with his pods.

"Yes," he whispered. Smiles spread over his two mouths. "Yes. Two empty glasses."

He turned to find that Morggul had stepped up to the bed. He was rocking on his short legs, studying the boy.

The boy slept soundly, silently on his back on top of the covers. He wore only pyjama bottoms. One pyjama leg had rolled up. His arms were crossed over his bare chest.

"Morggul—come away," Gobbul called in a loud whisper. "Don't wake him. Come away from there. We've seen all we need to see. We know that he drank the formula."

"But, Gobbul—" Morggul protested. "Something is wrong! Something is terribly wrong!" He waved frantically for Gobbul to join him.

"Sssssshhh," Gobbul hissed. "What is the matter?"

"The boy—" Morggul gasped, his face creased in horror. "He . . . isn't breathing!"

Gobbul's mouths opened in alarm. He pulled his body quickly over to the bed.

Did the formula kill the boy?

Morggul bent over the bed, staring at Nathan's bare arms. "Do you see?" he whispered. "Not breathing!"

Gobbul leaned closer. He studied the boy for a long moment. Then he shut his eyes.

When he opened them, his expression was angry. "Morggul, you fool!" he rasped. "Humans do not breathe through their tentacles as we do."

Morggul raised himself and turned to his leader. He made a wet, swallowing sound. "Huh? They don't?"

"Humans breathe through those two holes on their faces," Gobbul explained. "Look carefully. The boy is breathing steadily."

The fat alien turned back to the bed, leaned close to the boy's face, and watched him breathe. "Revolting," he murmured.

He raised his tentacles and sucked in large amounts of air through his purple pods. "Humans are so horrible and disgusting."

Gobbul nodded in agreement. "But if we can smarten up the boy and his sister," he whispered, "then they will be what we came looking for—young and strong *and* clever. They will make excellent slaves for our leader."

"And if the formula doesn't work?" Morggul asked. "If it doesn't make them cleverer?"

Two smiles played over Gobbul's face. "Then, Morggul, you can kill them and eat their hearts," he whispered. "My treat."

A thick gob of yellow drool ran down Morggul's chins and spattered on the carpet at his feet. "How long do they have to get clever enough?" he asked hungrily. "How long will we give them?"

"Not long," Gobbul whispered. "Let's give them a week. Maybe two. Then ... they are dinner."

6

"Nathan! Lindy! Rise and shine! Rise and shine!"

Mrs Nichols's voice rang through the house as it did every school morning.

Nathan yawned and stretched his bare arms over his head. He shivered. "Cold in here," he murmured, his mouth dry from sleep.

He opened his eyes and remembered he couldn't find his pyjama shirt the night before. It wasn't in the pile of clothes he had tossed into the wardrobe. So he had slept without it.

"Rise and shine! Rise and shine, you two!"

How can Mum sound so cheerful every morning? Nathan wondered. He stretched his arms again and lowered his feet to the floor.

"Yuck!"

What did I step in?

He squinted down at the yellow gob under his right foot. It was warm and wet. Nathan gazed

31

up at the ceiling. Had something dripped down from the attic?

No.

He raised his foot and examined it. The thick yellow liquid stuck to his foot.

"Maybe I squashed some kind of bug," he murmured. A bug in the middle of winter? He hopped on one foot over to his chest-of-drawers and grabbed a hunk of tissues to wipe the gunk off.

"How's it going?" Lindy called in to him on her way to the bathroom.

"Not a good start," he replied.

The day didn't get any better on the school bus. Nathan took a seat by himself near the front. Lindy headed to the back to join Gail Matthews and Erika Jones and some other friends.

Nathan swung his rucksack on to his lap and stared out of the bus window. It was a grey winter day. Wisps of fog clung to the trees and hedges. Gathering clouds threatened snow.

Nathan turned and saw Ellen and Wardell in the seat across from him. He groaned to himself. They were showing off, as usual. Doing *The Times* crossword puzzle.

They asked each other every clue as loudly as possible so that everyone on the bus would see they were doing the puzzle.

No one else in our class can do that puzzle,

Nathan thought bitterly. It's much too hard. So Ellen and Wardell have to do it every morning on the bus to make us all feel like morons.

"Hey, Nathan!" Wardell's voice burst into his thoughts. "Nathan, can you help us with this one?"

Ellen grinned across the aisle at him. "We're stumped," she said.

Nathan squinted at them suspiciously. They want *my* help?

"It's a six-letter word," Wardell said, his eyes on the puzzle grid. "The clue is, *oafish and dull*."

"What kind of fish?" Nathan asked.

Ellen and Wardell laughed.

Nathan felt his face turning red. "That was a joke!" he declared quickly.

"Yeah. Right." Ellen rolled her eyes.

"Oafish and dull," Wardell repeated. "Can you think of anything? Six letters. We just can't get it."

They both shook their heads and frowned at the puzzle.

Nathan thought hard. Six letters ... six letters...

This is my big chance to look cool, he thought. They never asked me for help before.

He suddenly remembered the bottle of Brain Juice. How long would it take that stuff to start working?

I could really use some brainpower now, he

thought, thinking hard, repeating the clue over and over in his mind. If only Uncle Frank's formula would work *now*!

"Oafish and dull," Wardell repeated, watching Nathan.

"Uh . . . well. . ." Nathan blanked out. He couldn't think of anything.

"Oh, wait! I've got it!" Wardell cried. He lowered his pencil to the newspaper and started writing. "The answer is *Nathan*. N-A-T-H-A-N!"

He and Ellen tossed back their heads and laughed. Several other kids burst out laughing too.

With an angry sigh, Nathan slid low in his seat. He stared out the window at the fog-covered lawns, the heavy grey sky.

I'm soooo stupid, he thought. I'm such a moron.

I'm not even clever enough to know when kids are playing a joke on me.

I don't even know how to spell *oafish*! he thought miserably.

And then he heard Lindy's cry from the back of the bus. "I don't believe it!"

He turned to see his sister running up the aisle, her hands pressed against her cheeks, eyes wide with alarm. "Lindy? What's wrong?" he called.

"My rucksack! I left it at home! I left all my books, all my stuff at home!" She lurched up to the driver. "Can we go back? Can we turn around? I left my rucksack!"

"Sorry," the driver, a plump woman in a grey uniform with a toothpick dangling from her lips, muttered without turning around.

"But I need my stuff! I'll fail! I'll fail!" Lindy wailed at the top of her lungs.

"Sorry."

We're both so stupid, Nathan thought unhappily. It's a miracle that we get through a day.

At least today can't get any worse, he told himself.

He was wrong again.

"Nathan, would you like to tell the whole class what is so funny?" Mr Tyssling lowered the chalk to his side and turned from the blackboard to view Nathan sternly.

Everyone in the class also turned to stare.

Nathan tried to stop laughing. But his friend Eddie Frinkes had passed him the funniest, grossest drawing of Mr Tyssling with long black worms coming out of his nose.

PICK ME, Eddie had captioned the drawing. Eddie is an artist, Nathan thought. An artist!

But how stupid was it to burst out laughing like a hyena while the class was silent, watching Mr Tyssling write a long equation on the blackboard?

Really stupid.

Because now the teacher was striding across the room towards Nathan, his eyes locked on the drawing in Nathan's hand.

And now he grabbed the paper from Nathan's

hand and was admiring *PICK ME* close up.

Nathan swallowed hard and gazed up at Mr Tyssling. The teacher wasn't smiling.

The class grew even silenter than silent.

"Did you draw this?" Mr Tyssling asked Nathan in a voice just above a whisper.

"No," Nathan managed to reply. His face was burning. He knew it must be as red as a tomato.

"Well, who drew it?" Mr Tyssling demanded softly.

"Uh. . ." No way Nathan could squeal on a friend. "I don't know," he said.

"Is it supposed to be me?" the teacher asked.

"I . . . don't know," Nathan replied. And he burst out laughing. He couldn't hold it in.

Stupid. So stupid.

Everyone was laughing now. Everyone except Mr Tyssling.

He waited for the laughter to die down. Then he handed the drawing back to Nathan. "It isn't very good," he said. "My hair is longer than that. And my nose is a lot shorter."

Oh, wow. He's not going to give me a hard time, Nathan realized. He let out a sigh of relief.

Too soon.

"Since you're getting such a big kick out of the class today, Nathan," Mr Tyssling said, "why don't you go up to the blackboard and show everyone how to solve the equation."

"Huh? Me?"

Nathan's heart pounded as he climbed up from his desk and made his way to the front of the room. His eyes blurred behind his glasses as he stared at the equation. *It was a mile long!*

He scratched his head and started to read it from the beginning:

$$x = a - c + 125(x+y)\ldots$$

Once again, Nathan thought of the Brain Juice. Wasn't it time for it to start working?

Wouldn't it be wonderful to know how to solve this problem? Nathan asked himself. Wouldn't it be wonderful to solve it in front of Mr Tyssling and all the kids who thought he was a moron?

The Brain Juice. If only. . .

If only. . .

And then, staring at the chalky letters and numbers, Nathan suddenly felt different.

As if a wave of electricity had shot through him.

He could feel the hairs stand up on his arm. It suddenly appeared so clear. So perfectly clear. The numbers seemed to *leap* off the blackboard at him. Leap together as a single unit.

I can do this! he realized. I can do this equation!

"Well, Nathan?" he heard Mr Tyssling's voice, impatient, behind him.

Nathan's eyes swept over the shimmering, gleaming numbers and letters. "Would you like me to solve it for x or y?" he asked the teacher.

Laughter burst out across the classroom. Scornful laughter.

Nathan didn't care. "I'll solve it first for x," he announced.

He picked up a piece of chalk and began writing. Scribbling numbers and letters. Scratching them furiously across the board.

Row after row. Number after number.

He wrote so frantically he broke the stick of chalk. Half of it went flying across the room. But Nathan kept writing.

His heart pounded. He'd never felt this way before in his life!

Finally, he finished with a gasp. And turned grinning, to Mr Tyssling. "Well?" he demanded, pointing to his final solution. "Well? What do you think?"

Mr Tyssling gaped at Nathan's scribbles that covered the board—and his mouth dropped open in amazement.

The teacher ran both hands back through his thick, dark hair. His eyes swept over the blackboard.

"I'm amazed," he murmured. "I'm blown away."

Nathan grinned at him.

Mr Tyssling swallowed and narrowed his eyes at Nathan. "You didn't get *one* thing right!" he declared. "Not one part of it."

"Excuse me?" Nathan choked out.

The teacher shook his head. "You wrote and wrote and wrote. You really had me fooled, Nathan. I thought you knew what you were doing. But. . ." His voice trailed off.

"It's . . . wrong?" Nathan gulped. His voice cracked.

"Totally wrong," Mr Tyssling said sadly. "Wrong from beginning to end."

Nathan slumped, like a balloon deflating. At least no one is laughing, he told himself. They all feel too sorry for me.

Too sorry for the stupid boy

"Can anyone give Nathan a hand up here?" Mr Tyssling asked. "Lindy, can you help your brother with this problem?"

"No . . . I can't," Lindy replied quietly. "I . . . left my book at home this morning. I haven't read this chapter."

Hidden by tall bushes, two green faces peered into the classroom window from outside.

His mouths tight with disgust, Gobbul turned to his partner. "They are both stupid, stupid, stupid," he spat, through four rows of jagged teeth.

"I suppose the Brain Energizer Fluid doesn't work on humans," Morggul replied. He watched through the dust-smeared glass as Nathan trudged unhappily back to his seat.

"Humans are a low species," Gobbul muttered.

"Well . . . since the fluid isn't working," Morggul began, his eyes lighting up, "do we have to wait any longer? Can I kill them and eat their hearts now?"

Gobbul sighed. "Yes. Go ahead," he said. "Enjoy."

"The Brain Juice isn't working, Uncle Frank," Lindy moaned.

"We aren't any cleverer at all," Nathan agreed.

They were in Nathan's room. He had his phone pressed to his ear. Lindy was using the portable phone from downstairs.

"I told you to be patient," Uncle Frank said at the other end. He had to shout over the roar of some kind of lab machinery.

"But we drank it all, and nothing happened," Nathan insisted shrilly. "I had a *horrible* day in school, and—"

"We think maybe we got a little stupider," Lindy added. Hunched on top of the desk, she frowned at Nathan across the room.

"Brain Juice doesn't work overnight," Uncle Frank shouted. "You have to give it time to get into your bloodstream. I told you both—"

The roar stopped in the background.

"What was that noise? Some kind of lab experiment?" Lindy asked.

"No. The blender," Dr King replied. "I'm mixing up some carrot juice."

"Well—when will we get cleverer?" Lindy demanded. "The maths test is tomorrow, and we were hoping we'd be able to get a good mark."

"Or at least *pass* it," Nathan groaned.

"Of *course* you'll pass it," Uncle Frank replied. "Don't you remember my instructions? You're supposed to work harder than you ever worked. And don't think about the Brain Juice. You'll see. It will work. You'll do fine on the test tomorrow."

"But . . . shouldn't it be in our bloodstreams already?" Nathan asked, scratching his curly hair.

"Forget about the Brain Juice. Just go and work," their uncle instructed. "Phone me tomorrow. I bet you will have good news for me."

They thanked him and said good-bye.

"Good news," Nathan muttered bitterly. He kicked his rucksack across the floor. "How can we have good news? We don't understand a single thing about these maths equations."

Lindy sighed. "I don't even know what chapters to revise."

"Maybe we should call one of the clever kids," Nathan suggested. "Maybe Ellen or Wardell or someone would come over and revise for the test with us."

"Are you kidding?" Lindy sneered. "Those kids would never study with us. They'd be afraid our stupidity would rub off on them!"

"I suppose..." Nathan replied sadly. He kicked his rucksack again. "Yikes! I hurt my toe!"

Lindy slid off the desktop and straightened the bottom of her sweater. "Well, let's get started. You heard what Uncle Frank said. We've got to work."

"You get out the maths book," Nathan replied. "And the revision sheet. I'll go down and get a couple of Cokes."

Lindy grabbed his rucksack and started to unzip it. Nathan headed past her, out into the hall.

He turned the corner to the stairway—

—and cried out as a sharp pain shot into his chest.

"Owwww! My heart!"

Nathan grabbed his chest and sank back against the wall.

He glared down at his sister. "Brenda—you hit me with that dart!"

Brenda nodded and laughed gleefully.

"Where did you get the darts? You're not allowed to play with darts!" Nathan cried angrily. "You—you could have *killed* me!"

"They're only sucker darts," Brenda replied.

"It really hurt! You hit me in the chest!" Nathan complained.

"That's fifty points," Brenda said, picking the dart up from the hall floor. "The head is a hundred points, stomach is fifty points, arms and legs are ten points."

"Just go away," Nathan groaned, rubbing his chest. "You're not funny. You're a total pain."

"Don't you want to play?" Brenda asked. She held up a sucker dart for him.

"No way!" he replied angrily. "Go away,

45

Brenda. I have a maths test to revise for."

He turned and stamped away.

And let out a loud cry of pain as a dart slammed hard into his back.

"Fifty points!" Brenda declared.

The next day, Lindy came up to Nathan after the maths test. "The test wasn't so hard," she said.

Nathan shrugged. "At least I got all the way through it. That's a good sign."

"I had to guess a few times," Lindy confessed. "And the third equation had me totally confused. But I tried to solve it anyway."

"I might have passed it," Nathan said. "Maybe. I'm not sure."

Behind them, they heard Wardell talking to Stan. "Too easy," he said.

"I aced it too," Stan replied.

They slapped each other a high five.

"Can't you make them any harder?" Wardell called to Mr Tyssling.

"Maybe next time," the teacher called back.

"How did you do, Nathan?" Wardell asked, grinning.

"Great!" Nathan replied quickly. "Awesome!" He flashed them a thumbs-up.

Wardell and Stan left the room laughing.

"I'm going to give back your maths tests now," Mr Tyssling announced the next afternoon. He walked through the rows of desks, handing out the test papers.

"Overall, I'm very pleased," he said. "It was a very hard test, and most of you did very well."

He stopped at Stan's desk. "Good job, Stan," he murmured. "Impressive work. And I liked the work you added for extra credit."

How did I do? Nathan wondered, clasping and unclasping his hands on his desktop. Did I pass? That's all I want. I just want to *pass* this one.

He glanced at Lindy across the room. She had both hands in her hair, nervously tangling and untangling strands.

Please. Please, let us both pass, Nathan prayed.

Mr Tyssling finished handing back the test papers.

"Uh . . . I didn't get mine," Nathan called out in a trembling voice.

Mr Tyssling turned and his smile faded. "Yes, I know, Nathan," he said sharply. "I need to see you and Lindy after school."

Oh, no, Nathan thought. Oh, nooooooo.

This is bad news. Very bad news.

After school, Mr Tyssling waited for the room to clear out. Then he called Nathan and Lindy to his desk. Gripping their test papers, he frowned at them.

"I'm sorry, you two," he said softly. "But I'm very disappointed in you both."

Nathan sighed. Lindy lowered her eyes to the floor.

"We—we failed?" Nathan asked in a tiny voice.

Mr Tyssling didn't reply. He strode angrily to the window and stared out at the cloudy grey sky.

"I suppose it's partly my fault," he said, his back to them. "I put a lot of pressure on you two to do well on this test."

He spun round to face them. "But I never dreamed that you would cheat!" he declared.

"Huh?"

"Cheat?"

"You both got perfect marks," the teacher said, holding up the test papers. "You solved every problem." He tossed the papers at them. "Why did you do it? Did you think cheating was the only way to impress me?"

"But—but we *didn't*!" Nathan cried.

"We just worked really hard," Lindy explained.

And we drank Brain Juice, she thought. But she couldn't tell the teacher that.

Wow, Lindy said to herself, her eyes sweeping down the perfect test paper. Wow. Wow. Does the Brain Juice really work? Are Nathan and I really clever now?

She raised her eyes to the teacher. "I like you two," he was saying. "So I'm not going to send you down to the head. I'm going to give you one more chance."

"But—but—but—" Nathan sputtered.

"We didn't cheat. Really!" Lindy protested.

Mr Tyssling rolled his eyes. He raised a finger to his lips. "Sshhh. It's okay. I understand why you did it. Look. I'm going to tear up these tests and give you a different one tomorrow."

"But—but—"

"Study really hard tonight, you two," he said. "I'm sure you can do well enough to pass. And we'll forget this ever happened."

Nathan and Lindy practically *skipped* the whole way home.

"We're geniuses! Geniuses!" Nathan declared gleefully.

"Uncle Frank is the genius," Lindy corrected him. "He made us smart. Just think, Nathan.

He can sell Brain Juice and make everyone in the world clever!"

"I don't care about everyone in the world," Nathan declared. "I only care about us! Do you realize how awesome it will be to get straight A's?"

"Whoa." Lindy's smile faded. "Maybe it's too early to talk about straight A's. Maybe we just got lucky on that test. Remember, we have to take another one tomorrow."

"We'll ace that one too!" Nathan exclaimed. "We don't even have to revise." With a loud, joyful *WHOOOOP*, he tossed his rucksack high in the air and caught it. They raced the rest of the way home.

Brenda was playing in the living room when they entered. She was down on the floor moving around the plastic pieces of the dolls' house.

"Are you still fooling around with that thing?" Lindy asked.

"No one will put it together for me," Brenda pouted. "Mum and Dad are too busy. And you and Nathan are too stupid."

"I'll do it for you," Nathan volunteered. He dropped down beside Brenda.

"No. I'll do it," Lindy insisted.

"We can both build it," Nathan said. He picked up the big instruction sheet and began ripping it into pieces.

"Stop it! What are you *doing*?" Brenda cried, trying to grab it away from him.

Nathan laughed. "We don't need the instructions."

He and Lindy began sliding pieces together. The living room rang out with the *CLICK CLICK CLICK* of plastic tab A fitting into plastic slot B.

A few minutes later, the walls and floors and roof had all been fitted together. Brenda gaped in amazement at the finished dolls' house. "How did you do that?" she cried.

"Easy," Lindy replied.

"We're geniuses," Nathan added.

He and Lindy tossed back their heads and laughed in sheer happiness.

After dinner, Nathan and Lindy were sprawled on the floor of the TV room, watching *Jeopardy*. Mr and Mrs Nichols sat behind them on the sofa, reading magazines.

"Who was Queen Victoria?" Lindy shouted.

"Who was Isabella of Spain?" Nathan shouted, a few seconds later.

And Lindy, a few seconds later, "Who was George the Third of England?"

Mrs Nichols looked up from her magazine. "You're calling out the answers?"

"Ssshhh," Lindy replied, leaning closer to the TV. "The category is Monarchs in History."

"But how do you know all those?" her mum demanded.

"What is the element zinc?" Nathan shouted out.

"What is iron?" Lindy answered the next one. "They changed the category," she told her mother.

"But how do you know chemical elements?" Mrs Nichols demanded. "And—you're calling out the answers before he even *asks* the questions!"

"They're fooling you," Mr Nichols chimed in, lowering his magazine. "They've seen this programme before. It's a repeat. That's how they know all the right answers."

"Is that true?" Lindy's mum asked. "You've seen this show before?"

"No. We haven't seen it," Lindy replied, without turning around. "Ssshh."

"What is the Spanish Armada?" Nathan called to the TV screen.

"What is the *Lusitania*?" he and Lindy both shouted in unison.

"We've cleared the board!" Nathan exclaimed. "We got every answer right."

They both pumped their fists over their heads as their parents looked on in astonishment.

"We're ready for Final Jeopardy!" Lindy declared.

*

"Final Jeopardy," Gobbul murmured, watching the two kids through the window, hidden by the darkness of the winter evening. "Final Jeopardy. Yes, I think that describes what those two human kids are about to face."

Morggul bobbed up and down on his fat, wet body, peering through the fogged-up window.

"I am so glad I changed my mind," Gobbul said. "So glad I decided not to let you eat them."

A sly smile spread over Gobbul's mouths. "Yes. Now they are young and strong—and smart enough. Morggul," he whispered, "I think we have found our slaves."

"Uncle Frank, you won't believe it!" Lindy declared into the telephone.

She could hear her uncle chuckle at the other end of the line. "*What* won't I believe?"

"Nathan and I got perfect scores on the maths test!" Lindy exclaimed excitedly. "The drink you gave us—it worked!"

Uncle Frank laughed heartily. "Maybe your revision and hard work had something to do with it," he suggested.

"No. We're geniuses!" Nathan declared, grabbing the phone from Lindy. "The Brain Juice made us geniuses! You have to bottle it, Uncle Frank. You have to sell it in shops. You'll make a fortune!"

"Well . . . I'm glad it helped you," their uncle replied. "But don't forget to keep working hard. That's the most important thing."

Dr King chatted with the two excited kids a while longer. Then he hung up and turned to his wife. "They got perfect scores on their maths test," he said, chuckling. "This shows what a little *confidence* will do for kids. I gave them a bottle of grape juice to drink, and now they think they are *geniuses*!"

The next morning, Lindy stopped Nathan before they climbed on to the school bus. "Don't show off," she warned him. "Really. You have to act cool. We don't want everyone to know what's happened to us."

But Nathan couldn't act cool about his new brainpower. He had waited *so long* to be one of the smart kids.

He watched Wardell and Ellen across the aisle, showing off as usual, working on *The Times* crossword puzzle. He waited for them to turn to him.

"Hey, Nathan," Wardell called out with that superior smirk on his face. "What's a six-letter word for dumb-bell? It begins with an N."

Ellen giggled. Several other kids laughed.

"Let me see that," Nathan said. He grabbed the folded-up newspaper from Wardell's hand. He lowered his eyes to the puzzle.

"What are you doing?" Ellen demanded. "Give that back."

"I think I can help you," Nathan replied. He pulled out a ballpoint pen—and, writing as quickly as he could, filled in every word in the puzzle—*in ink*!

"Huh? Let me see that!" Wardell cried. He grabbed the paper back. He and Ellen studied the puzzle, their faces twisted in shock.

Ellen eyed Nathan suspiciously. "How did you do that?"

Nathan shrugged. "Crosswords are easy, if you have a good vocabulary."

Later that morning, Mr Tyssling gave them the maths test while the rest of the class worked on reading projects. "Take your time," he instructed them. "And leave out any problems you have trouble with."

Nathan and Lindy took the tests back to their desks.

"And be sure to show your work, kids," Mr Tyssling added. "I want to see what you understand and what you don't. Then we can work extra hard on the things you don't understand."

Nathan and Lindy nodded.

Ten minutes later, Lindy carried her test paper up to Mr Tyssling. It took Nathan *twelve* minutes because he worked out one of the problems three different ways.

Mr Tyssling gazed up at them in surprise. "What's wrong?" he asked. "Are the problems too hard for you?"

He gazed quickly through their papers. His expression changed.

He studied their answers again, reading more slowly.

"P-perfect marks again!" he stammered. "I'm really impressed. You two must have revised really hard."

"We didn't revise at all," Nathan bragged. "Maths is easy."

After school, Nathan and Lindy played a game of catch with Brenda in the back garden. The sun had come out after weeks of grey skies. The air felt warm, more like spring than winter.

"I did all my homework before the end of school," Lindy told Nathan. She bounced the rubber ball over the grass to her little sister.

Brenda missed. She chased the ball to the hedge in front.

"I did tomorrow's homework too," Nathan replied. "I memorized the poetry book."

"I finished all the problems in the maths workbook for the rest of the year," Lindy said, catching Brenda's throw. She bounced the ball back to Brenda.

"Me too," Nathan told her. "We'll have to ask him for extra work. Maybe we can start on next year's maths."

Brenda threw the ball hard. Nathan wasn't looking, and it bounced off his chest. Brenda tossed back her head and giggled.

Lindy grabbed the ball and rolled it across the

yard to Brenda. "You've got to stop correcting Mr Tyssling," she scolded Nathan. "Every time he made a mistake today, your hand shot up."

"Well, he made too many mistakes," Nathan grumbled. "He spelled *Massachusetts* wrong on the blackboard. Somebody had to tell him."

"But, Nathan—"

"And the Articles of Confederation were signed in 1781—not 1778," Nathan continued. "How could he *make* a mistake like that?"

"Kids began to groan every time you raised your hand," Lindy warned him. "I really think you should keep your corrections to yourself. Even Mr Tyssling was starting to look annoyed."

"Get the ball!" Brenda's cry interrupted Lindy's lecture. "Get the ball!" Brenda called, pointing. "It went into the bushes."

Nathan spotted the ball under a clump of evergreen bushes along the wall of the house. He started to run to the bushes—and then stopped.

"Hey, Lindy—look." He pointed down to the ground in front of him.

Lindy hurried over. "What?"

"Weird footprints," Nathan said.

"Get the ball! Get the ball!" Brenda cried impatiently.

"In a minute," Nathan called. He squatted down to examine the deep ruts in the winter-hard ground.

"Wow," Lindy murmured beside him. "The

prints are so big. And so round. What kind of animal makes footprints like these?"

Nathan shook his head. He moved to the next print. Then the next. "Eight toes," he announced. "Look. More than one set of prints. And they seem to be heading up to the house."

"It's not a dog or a cat," Lindy said fretfully. "It must be something really big and heavy. Look how deep the footprints are."

"Eight toes," Nathan repeated. "Eight toes. Weird."

They followed the line of prints to the house. They appeared to lead up to the window. "The bushes—" Nathan cried out. "The bushes are all trampled."

"See the ball?" Brenda called, jumping up and down impatiently. "Throw me the ball."

Nathan reached under the flattened bush for the ball. "Yuck!" He jerked his hand out.

"What's that slimy stuff?" Lindy demanded.

Nathan held his hand up. Thick yellow slime oozed over his fingers. "Oh, wow. It smells awful!" he moaned.

He dropped to his knees. And saw wet puddles of slime under the den window. Brenda's ball had rolled into one of the puddles.

"There are smears on the window," Lindy declared. "Look. Two smears. Like some creatures pushed their faces against the glass."

Nathan climbed to his feet. He examined the

sticky goo on his fingers. Then he raised his eyes to the smears on the window. "Do you think some animals were *watching* us?"

"But what *were* they?" Lindy cried. "Why were they here? Why were they outside our window?"

She shivered. "I'm scared, Nathan. I'm really scared."

A week later, Nathan stood at his locker, filling up his rucksack, preparing to go home after school. "Hey, how's it going?" he called to his friend Eddie Frinkes at a locker across the hall.

Eddie nodded.

"Want to come hang out at my house and play computer games?" Nathan asked.

Eddie made a face. "No. I don't think so."

"Come on. Why not?" Nathan pleaded.

Eddie shrugged. "I can't play any games with you. You're too good. You always win."

"But—" Nathan started.

Eddie slammed his locker shut and hurried away.

Before Nathan could chase after him, Stan and Wardell and three other boys came round the corner. They stopped when they saw Nathan and formed a circle around him.

"Hey, Nathan—recite the poetry book for us!" Stan said with a sneer.

"Tell us some Greek myths!" Wardell demanded.

"Tell us about all the mistakes you found in the maths book!"

"Tell us how you reprogrammed all the computers in the computer lab!"

"Give me a break," Nathan pleaded.

"Did you really memorize the whole history book?" a kid asked.

"Well ... yes." Nathan could feel his face growing hot. "I read it, and it just kind of stayed with me."

"Are you really doing ten book reports for extra credit?" Stan demanded, pushing up against Nathan menacingly.

"Well ... maybe." Nathan tried to back away. But he was already up against the lockers. "Hey—give that back!" he cried as Wardell grabbed his rucksack.

Wardell spun round and took off down the corridor, holding Nathan's rucksack in front of him. Laughing, the other guys went running after him. "You're such a brain," Wardell called. "Figure out how to get it back!"

Nathan sighed and started after them. But he stopped when he saw Lindy come slumping round the corner. Her auburn hair was tangled and fell in clumps over her forehead. Her eyes were red-rimmed.

"Lindy, what's wrong? Were you crying?" he demanded, hurrying over to her.

"I suppose so." She turned away, embarrassed. Her chest was heaving up and down. It took her a few seconds to catch her breath.

"What happened?" Nathan asked softly.

"Oh . . . it's Gail and Erika," Lindy choked out. "They . . . they don't want to be friends with me any more."

"Huh?" Nathan gasped. "They're your best friends. What is their problem?"

"They said I'm a freak," Lindy told him, her voice breaking. "They said I'm too weird now that I'm so clever. They said . . . they said they're *afraid* of me!"

"But that's stupid!" Nathan protested. "Just because you're clever—"

He stopped in midsentence. And stared across the hall.

"Huh?"

He and Lindy both gasped in shock as two figures stepped quickly from the shadows.

"Mum! Dad! What are *you* doing here?" Lindy cried.

Their parents crossed the hall towards them, their expressions grim.

Nathan felt his stomach tighten in dread. "Is something wrong?"

"Maybe *you* can answer that question," Mr Nichols replied, eyeing Nathan sternly. "Mr Tyssling called your mum and me in for a meeting."

"Are you two in trouble?" Mrs Nichols asked.

"Trouble? No. I don't think so," Nathan replied, thinking hard.

"We haven't done anything!" Lindy protested shrilly.

"Well, come with us," Mr Nichols said. "We're supposed to meet in Mrs Lopez's office."

"Mrs Lopez?" Nathan cried. "Why do we have to meet with the head? What's going on?"

A few seconds later, they stepped into the

front office. The front room was empty. It was nearly four o'clock, and the secretaries had gone home.

Mrs Lopez greeted them at the door to the back office. She was a short, plump woman with black hair piled high on her head. Kids liked her because she had a warm, friendly smile and knew the name of every kid in school.

But she wasn't smiling now, Nathan noticed. She led them all inside and motioned for them to take seats at the long wooden table in the centre of the room.

Mr Tyssling was already seated at one end. He stood up and greeted Mr and Mrs Nichols. Then he introduced Mr Haywood, the school guidance counsellor.

Mr Haywood nodded solemnly to Nathan and Lindy. He was a pale, balding man, straight as a needle, who seemed to wear the same grey suit and thin blue tie every day.

Mrs Lopez closed the office door behind her and stepped up behind the chair at the head of the table. "Thank you for coming in, Mr and Mrs Nichols," she said. "I'm afraid we have a strange problem on our hands."

"Problem?" Mrs Nichols asked. She frowned across the table at Nathan and Lindy.

"Have these two been acting up?" Mr Nichols demanded.

Mrs Lopez slid into the chair and pulled it up

to the long table. She clasped her pudgy hands in front of her on the tabletop. "No. It's not a discipline problem," she replied.

The head glanced at Nathan and Lindy. "I don't know quite how to begin," she said. "But I suppose I should just say it."

Mr Tyssling fiddled with a loose thread on his sweater sleeve. Mr Haywood cleared his throat and shifted uncomfortably in his chair.

"Nathan and Lindy are upsetting the other kids," Mrs Lopez began. "And I'm afraid they're upsetting their teachers too."

"But—wait!" Nathan started.

Mrs Lopez raised a hand to silence him. "Your two kids appear to be geniuses," she continued. "We don't know why we didn't realize this sooner. But in the past couple of weeks, it has become very clear."

"Geniuses?" Mr Nichols rubbed his chin, staring at Nathan and Lindy.

Mrs Lopez nodded. "They get perfect marks on every exam and test. They've memorized all of their textbooks. They read book after book after book. They write twenty-page essays for extra credit."

"But ... that's *wonderful!*" Mrs Nichols declared. "I know they've been working really hard every night."

"I regret to say it isn't wonderful," Mrs Lopez replied softly. "Nathan and Lindy are constantly correcting their teachers. They find mistakes in the textbooks. The other kids are very upset by their actions. They feel they cannot compete with Nathan and Lindy. I believe other kids feel that something weird, something . . . unnatural is going on."

"Nathan and Lindy don't mean to cause trouble," Mr Tyssling chimed in, leaning forward over the table. "But they can't help it. They know too much. Much more than any other twelve-year-olds on the planet! And this is ruining school for everyone else."

"I've noticed that kids stay away from them," Mr Haywood added. "I'm sorry to say it—but I think a lot of our students are *afraid* of Nathan and Lindy."

Suddenly, Nathan realized that all eyes were on Lindy and him. Nathan's heart pounded. Is this really happening? he wondered. Are we really in trouble because we're too smart?

A chill ran down his back and made him shudder.

Am I some kind of freak? he asked himself.

I have no friends. The kids all hate me.

And I guess the teachers hate me too.

What is going to happen to me?

He glanced at Lindy. Her head was lowered. Her hands were clasped tightly in her lap. He knew she must be having the same sad, frightening thoughts.

"We can explain it!" Lindy cried, suddenly snapping back to life. "We can explain it all."

"Lindy, wait—" Nathan grabbed her arm. "We promised Uncle Frank we wouldn't tell anyone."

"We *have* to tell!" Lindy insisted. She pulled her arm free.

"Tell us *what*?" her mum demanded.

"We drank Brain Juice!" Lindy blurted out.

"Lindy, please—" Nathan begged.

But Lindy wouldn't be stopped. "Uncle Frank gave us a bottle of Brain Juice. To help us get cleverer. We drank it—and ... it worked. The Brain Juice turned us into geniuses!"

Mrs Nichols' mouth dropped open. Mr Nichols narrowed his eyes at Lindy, studying her in silence.

Everyone remained silent for a long moment.

Then Mrs Lopez broke the silence with a sigh. "I don't know what kind of magic formula turned you two into geniuses," she said softly. "But I know one thing for sure. You have to leave this school. We cannot have you here any longer."

A few days later, Nathan and Lindy sat glumly in the TV room, watching themselves on the TV news.

"These two kids are in a battle with the school board," the reporter was saying. "Are they too clever to go to school? The school says yes. Their parents say no. And so the fight continues. . ."

Behind him, Nathan could hear his stepmum on the phone in the hall. "Well, our lawyer says we have a good chance," she was saying. "Of course, we're looking into private schools too. No. No . . . their Uncle Frank is in Sweden with his wife. Out in the wilderness. No way to reach him."

The front doorbell chimed.

Nathan jumped up to answer it—but stopped.

Probably another reporter, wanting to ask the same questions. He and Lindy had been interviewed at least a dozen times!

He always thought it would be exciting and

fun to be interviewed on TV and radio. But it wasn't fun at all. Not when people thought you were freaks.

Not when you had to stay home from school because people didn't want you there. Not when you didn't have any friends to watch you on TV.

That Brain Juice ruined my whole life, Nathan thought bitterly. And now, everyone in the world knows about it!

He crept into the front hall and listened to his stepmum arguing with the woman at the front door. "No. No way," she was telling the woman. "We're not interested in a Brain Juice fruit drink. Yes. Yes. I'm sure your company makes very good, healthy drinks. But my kids don't want to sell drinks on TV advertisements."

Nathan slunk back into the TV room. Over the drone of the TV, he could still hear his stepmum arguing with the woman.

"Who is out there?" Lindy asked lifelessly.

"Someone else who wants us to sell something," Nathan groaned.

The day before, a man came to the house, saying he wanted to be their agent. He had big plans—a Clever Kids line of trainers, a Brain-Treat candy bar, Sugar Corn Clever cereal... Maybe a Saturday morning cartoon show.

"We can make a *fortune*!" Nathan had cried. "We'll be famous!"

"But we'll be famous freaks," Lindy had

70

complained. "People will point at us. And make jokes about us. We'll never be normal again."

"But we'll be rich!" Nathan argued.

Tears brimmed in Lindy's eyes. "I . . . I just want to go back to school," she wailed. "I just want to have my friends again."

The family decided to wait. To be careful. Not to sign up for anything, at least until the school fight was settled.

But that didn't stop people from calling. Reporters . . . agents . . . salespeople . . . kids who wanted help with their homework . . . strange people who said they were desperate and needed advice—needed someone smart to tell them what to do.

And later that afternoon, Nathan and Lindy were amusing Brenda in the back garden when a black truck pulled up the driveway. They stopped their Frisbee game to watch two tall, dark-suited men stride up to the front door.

Nathan dropped the Frisbee to the grass and followed Lindy to the house to see what they wanted.

"Mrs Nichols, we spoke to your husband about the tests," one of the men was saying.

"Tests?" Mrs Nichols frowned.

"Yes," the man replied. "We're from the university research lab in town. We need to take your son and daughter to the lab. We want to give them a round of tests. Intelligence tests. Other tests."

The other man glanced at Nathan and Lindy. "We want to see just how clever you kids are. Maybe you could be useful in the government. You'd like to serve your country, wouldn't you?"

Nathan and Lindy didn't reply. They just stared back at the two grim-faced men.

"I—I'm not sure about this." Their mum hesitated.

"We will only need them for a few hours," one of the men replied. "We'll give them the written tests. Then they'll be interviewed by some doctors. Oh. And, of course, the surgery."

"Surgery?" Mrs Nichols cried.

"Yes. We need to take a few samples of brain tissue."

"No way!" Nathan and Lindy cried in unison.

They both spun away from the front steps and ran across the garden.

"Hey—aren't you going to throw the Frisbee?" Brenda called after them.

They didn't turn back. Running side by side, they leaped over the low hedge that divided their yard from the next—and kept going.

Past the neighbours' house, they turned sharply and headed to the back. Nathan could hear the two men calling after them. He lowered his head like a football fullback and ploughed through a narrow opening in the neighbours' tall fence.

Without slowing, without saying a word, Nathan and Lindy tore through back gardens. Then down a narrow alley. Across the street that led towards the main street of the town. And through more back gardens.

Finally, four or five streets from home, they

stopped, gasping for breath. Nathan bent over, pressed his hands against his knees, and struggled to catch his breath.

"Where are we?" Lindy choked out. "Are those two men coming after us?"

Nathan glanced around. "No. I don't think so." The grey shingle house ahead of them looked familiar. "Hey—that's Wardell's house!"

Without hesitating, they ran up to the back door. Nathan pounded on the glass. "Hey—anybody home?"

A few seconds later, Wardell pulled open the door, his eyes wide with surprise. "Hey—what's up?" he asked.

"Can we come in?" Lindy asked breathlessly. She glanced behind her. "Someone may be chasing us."

"Well . . . yeah." Wardell stepped back to allow them in. Ellen and Stan were at the kitchen table, which was cluttered with books and papers. They both looked up in surprise.

"Lock the door!" Lindy instructed Wardell.

"What's going on?" Wardell demanded.

Nathan shrugged. He unzipped his jacket. Despite the cold of the day, his forehead was drenched with sweat.

"We had to get away," Lindy said. "It's a little crazy at our house right now."

They walked over to the table. "What's up?" Nathan asked, gazing at the papers and books.

An awkward silence. "Studying for the history test," Ellen finally replied. "It's a tough one. It covers the whole term."

Stan blew a large pink bubblegum bubble, then sucked it back into his mouth. "You two coming back to school?" he asked.

"Maybe," Nathan answered.

"We don't know," Lindy said.

Another awkward silence.

Nathan jammed his hands into his jeans pockets. "Uh . . . what's going on at school?" he asked.

"Nothing much," Wardell said. He was still staring at them as if they were Martians.

"Same old stuff," Ellen muttered.

"I saw you on the news," Stan said. "That was pretty cool." He blushed. "Actually, I mean . . . I thought you got a bad deal."

"Yeah. Me too," Ellen said softly, lowering her eyes to the table.

"We really want to come back," Lindy told them.

"I can't believe Mrs Lopez did that," Ellen said, shaking her head.

"Want a Coke or something?" Wardell asked, moving to the refrigerator. "I've got apple juice."

"Maybe we should use your phone and call home," Nathan said, gazing out the kitchen window.

"Yeah. Sure," Wardell said. He pointed to the

phone on the kitchen wall. "You know . . . uh. . ." He hesitated.

Nathan and Lindy waited.

"Sorry if I gave you a hard time in school," Wardell muttered, speaking rapidly. "I really didn't mean anything. I was just fooling around. You know."

"No problem," Nathan told him. "It wasn't your fault we got kicked out of school and our lives got so messed up." His voice broke.

He suddenly felt so sad, so upset.

It's nice being with friends, he thought. Being normal.

What if those men really do take us to their lab and slice open our brains? Then what?

He grabbed the phone off the wall and called home. His stepmum answered on the second ring. "Nathan—where are you?" she demanded. "Is Lindy with you?"

"We're at Wardell's house," he replied. "Are they gone? The men from the lab? Did they leave?"

"Of course they left," she replied. "I told them to go away."

"You mean . . . they're not going to cut open our brains?"

"No. No one is going to touch your brains," she assured him. "Why did you run away like that? You knew I would never let those men take you away."

76

"I . . . I suppose we just panicked," Nathan stammered. He turned round. Wardell, Stan, and Ellen were all staring at him.

"We'll be right home," he told his stepmum.

"Yes. Hurry," she said. "I need you to take care of Brenda. Dad and I have to go and see the school board."

"Okay. See you in a few minutes."

He replaced the phone on the wall. "Everything is okay," he told Lindy. "They're gone. Come on."

He started to the door. "Thanks, Wardell."

"See you two," Wardell replied.

"Wish we could revise with you," Lindy said sadly.

"Good luck," Ellen called.

"Yeah. Good luck," Stan and Wardell echoed.

Zipping up their jackets against the cold wind, Nathan and Lindy made their way out of the kitchen door and began jogging side by side through the back gardens and alleys.

They were halfway home when two aliens stepped out from a hedge to block their way.

Nathan stopped short as the two creatures stepped forward. Lindy had her eyes on the ground and nearly ran into them.

Nathan grabbed her arm and tugged her to a stop.

Lindy finally looked up—and let out a scream of terror.

Nathan opened his mouth to scream—but the sound choked in his throat.

They're so . . . *ugly*! he thought. I've never seen *anything* so ugly!

The big green creatures moved closer. Their yellow eyes glistened wetly. Their double mouths writhed and twitched with excitement. And as the mouths opened, Nathan saw four rows of jagged teeth.

Their shimmering, wet tentacles uncoiled rapidly and spread out to trap Nathan and Lindy. The tentacles were covered with disgusting purple pods that opened and closed like mouths.

The taller one had curled tusks. He licked them excitedly with two fat purple tongues. The fatter one bobbed up and down on his stumpy legs, his green belly slapping the grass.

"Wh-who are you?" Nathan choked out. "Are those . . . costumes?"

Lindy huddled close to Nathan, her eyes wide with fright. They both watched gobs of sweat slide off the sleek green bodies on to the grass.

"Why would we wear costumes?" the fatter one asked his partner.

The tusked one shook his head. "We do not come from your planet," he said, yellow eyes trained on Nathan. "So we do not look like you."

"Thank goodness!" his companion muttered.

Lindy's mouth dropped open. "This is a joke—right?" she whispered to Nathan. "Please—"

Nathan stared straight ahead. Trembling, he studied the two bobbing, sweating creatures. "No joke," he whispered back. "They're . . . real!"

Nathan took a deep breath. "We have to get home," he told them, trying to sound strong. But his voice cracked on the words.

"No. You will not be going home," the tall one replied softly. His tongues lapped at his tusks.

"What do you *mean*?" Lindy cried, her voice rising in fear. "What do you want? Who are you?"

"We are your new masters," the tall one replied flatly, speaking with his top mouth.

"You are going to be good slaves for our emperor," the fatter one gurgled.

"Slaves?" Nathan stared at them, frantic thoughts whirring through his mind. "This is a joke—right?"

"We do not joke," the tall one replied coldly.

"If you come from another planet, how come you speak English?" Lindy demanded suspiciously.

"Your language is a crude, primitive language," the tall one said, sneering with both mouths. "It took us only an hour or two to learn it. It is so simple. *Our* alphabet has seven hundred letters!"

"Our language has four hundred words for *hello*," the fatter one bragged.

"They've got to be kidding," Lindy whispered. "Haven't they?"

Nathan didn't reply. His heart thudded in his chest. He had a heavy feeling of dread in the pit of his stomach.

"I don't believe it," he choked out. "I just don't believe it."

The fatter one glanced up at the tusked one. "Go ahead," the tusked one said. "Prove it to him. Show him that we really are from another planet."

Nathan gasped as the fatter one turned to the

tree behind him and whipped one of his tentacles into the air. The tentacle slapped a bird off the bottom branch.

The bird let out a squeak—as the fat creature wrapped a tentacle round it, raised it to his bottom mouth, and bit its head off.

He made a loud swallowing sound as the bird's head slid down his throat. Then he jammed the rest of the bird into his mouth and chewed. Feathers spilled over his chin and floated to the ground.

"Ohhhh, disgusting." Lindy let out a moan and buried her face in Nathan's jacket sleeve.

"Do you need any more proof?" the taller one asked.

He didn't wait for an answer.

With one quick motion, he slid out a hot, wet tentacle. Wrapped it tightly around Lindy. And began pulling her towards his open mouths.

"Nooooooo!"

Lindy's scream of horror echoed over the back gardens.

"Help us!" Nathan shrieked. "Somebody—help us!"

He dived at Lindy. With both hands, he made a desperate grab for the tentacle that held her. He squeezed his fingers round it—and tugged.

Tugged with all his strength.

His hands slipped on the sweaty, wet skin.

Slowly, the tentacle loosened and slid away from Lindy.

She staggered back a few steps, then dropped to her knees.

"You can get up. And stop carrying on like that. We're not going to eat you," the taller creature sneered.

"Not yet," the fatter one added, chuckling, bouncing up and down like a trained seal.

"We wouldn't waste our Brain Energizer

Fluid," the tall one announced. "You are now too smart for us to eat you."

"Excuse me?" Nathan cried breathlessly. Alien sweat stuck in thick gobs on his hands. He wiped them on the legs of his jeans.

"Brain—what?" Lindy gasped, climbing slowly to her feet. The tentacle left a wide wet spot around her coat.

"The liquid we gave you," the tusked one answered. "To make you cleverer."

"But Uncle Frank—" Lindy started.

Both creatures shook their smooth heads. "He gave you grape juice. We gave you the real thing."

"But—why?" Nathan choked out.

"To make you clever enough for the emperor," the tall one replied. "The emperor wants his slaves to be quick and sharp. He doesn't believe that humans can be smart enough to be slaves. He sent us here to see if it was possible."

"If you two work out well, we will come back to your planet," the other one said. "And we will take thousands and thousands of slaves." He pulled off a bird feather that clung to his chin.

"I am Gobbul," the tusked one announced. "And this is my helper, Morggul. We will be your masters until we deliver you to the emperor."

No, Nathan thought, gazing up at the two ugly alien creatures. No . . . no. . . . This can't be happening.

"You will come with us to our spacecraft," Gobbuls ordered. He pointed to the woods. The purple pods up and down his tentacles let out a whoosh of sour air. "It is a long journey to our planet. We must leave at once."

No . . . no. . . The word repeated in Nathan's mind.

He glanced at his stepsister. Lindy's hand squeezed Nathan's arm. She didn't even realize she was doing it. Her whole body trembled in terror.

No . . . no. . . I can't let this happen.

Think, Nathan, he ordered himself. Think of a plan. Think of a good plan to escape these creatures.

He took a deep breath and lowered his mouth to Lindy's ear. "*Run!*" he whispered.

She nodded.

They spun away from the aliens—and took off.

Nathan lurched forward. He ran about three steps—and felt a thick tentacle wrap around his left ankle.

"Noooo!" He let out a furious cry as he stumbled.

The tentacle tightened round his leg.

He fell forward. Fell hard to the ground. Landed on his elbows and knees.

"Nooo!" Pain shot through his body. But he ignored it and rolled on to his back.

He kicked out both legs. Kicked free of the pod-covered tentacle. Scrambled to his feet. And, gasping for breath, leaped over a clump of low bushes—and kept running.

He could see Lindy up ahead, running through winter-dead flower beds, leaping over a low fence, then charging down a narrow alley.

Running full speed, arms stretched in front of her as if grabbing for safety, her auburn hair flying behind her like a flag. Running in terror. Not looking back.

They both reached their back garden, gasping for breath, leg muscles throbbing, holding their sides.

Mrs Nichols stood on the back steps, car keys in one hand, the other hand pressed against her waist. "What took you so long?" she snapped.

"We . . . we. . ." Nathan struggled to speak. But his lungs felt about to burst!

"I *told* you I was in a hurry. I *told* you I needed you to watch Brenda," Mrs Nichols said angrily.

"M-monsters!" Lindy cried.

"Two aliens!" Nathan uttered breathlessly. "They want to *kidnap* us!"

Mrs Nichols scowled and shook her head. "You'll have to do better than that. There's no way I'm going to buy *that* excuse!"

"Mum—listen!" Lindy begged. "We're in trouble. We—"

"I *know* you're in trouble," her mother interrupted. "That's why I have to go and talk to the school board." She pointed to the house. "Get in there. Brenda is waiting for you. I'm terribly late."

"But—" Lindy protested.

Her mother disappeared into the car and slammed the door.

"Mum—we're not kidding!" Lindy wailed.

"They're going to take us away!" Nathan cried.

Mrs Nichols called out something through the windscreen. They saw her mouth moving. But they couldn't hear her.

"*Listen* to us!" Lindy pleaded.

But her mother turned her head and backed the car down the driveway.

With an unhappy sigh, Nathan opened the kitchen door and led the way into the house. He locked the door carefully behind him.

The kitchen smelled of chocolate. Mum must have been baking brownies, Nathan thought.

"Brenda, where are you?" he called.

"In here!"

Nathan started to follow her voice to the living room. But Lindy held him back. "What are we going to do?" she whispered frantically.

He shrugged. "I don't know. We have to think. But . . . let's not scare Brenda."

She nodded in agreement. "Maybe we can get her to watch a video or something. Then we can think. Think of a plan, someone to help us."

They stepped into the living room. Brenda was on her stomach on the floor, surrounded by her Barbie dolls. "Where were you?" she demanded. "I want you to play dolls with me."

"Well. . ." Nathan hesitated.

"We thought you might like to watch that new video," Lindy suggested. "The one about the girl who moves to—"

"No!" Brenda interrupted. "I *told* you. I want to play dolls."

"But Lindy and I—" Nathan started.

That's as far as he got.

He heard a loud *CRASH*. And knew at once what it was.

The sound of the kitchen door being smashed open.

"What was *that*?" Brenda cried.

No time to answer.

The two ugly aliens slid into the room. Their yellow eyes gazed at Nathan and Lindy. Eyes cold as ice. Their mouths were turned down in tight scowls.

"Yuck!" Brenda exclaimed. "Who are they?"

"Slaves, we need you to come with us," Gobbul boomed. "We don't plan to chase you all over this planet."

"No!" Lindy screeched.

"We're not going!" Nathan cried. "We're not!"

Gobbul sighed through all of his purple tentacle pods. "I suppose we will have to persuade you." He nodded to Morggul.

Morggul moved quickly. He bounced across the room and lifted Brenda off the floor in two tentacles.

"Put me down!" she wailed, kicking her legs, thrashing her arms, trying to hit the big creature. "Help, Nathan! Lindy! Make him put me down!"

Nathan started across the room to help Brenda.

But Gobbul swung a tentacle round Nathan's neck and started to tighten it.

Nathan stopped short. He struggled to breathe.

"What are you going to do?" Lindy shrieked.

"Persuade you to come peacefully with us," Gobbul replied calmly. He turned to Morggul. "Go ahead and eat the little one," he said.

Morggul's purple tongues slid out hungrily. Thick saliva splashed the floor. "Yes. Good!" he gurgled.

"Save me a leg," Gobbul said. "You know I like legs."

Brenda screamed and kicked.

But Morggul raised her easily over him. As he lowered her to his face, his mouths stretched wide . . . wider. . .

"Stop!" Nathan gasped. "Please!"

"Don't swallow her!" Lindy begged. "We'll go with you. Promise! We won't run. We'll go with you. Just don't eat her!"

A cruel grin spread over Gobbul's mouths. "Too late," he whispered.

The inside of the aliens' spaceship was silvery and bright, so bright Nathan and Lindy had to shield their eyes at first.

Squinting, Nathan saw dozens of small compartments. Like a honeycomb, he thought. Or the inside of a beehive.

Before he could see clearly, Gobbul and Morggul shoved Lindy and him into a small, square compartment. Shimmering silver bars formed the walls, floor, and ceiling. They heard the click of the door being locked.

"It's a cage," Lindy gasped. "They locked us in a cage."

The two aliens disappeared into a silvery passageway. Nathan and Lindy leaned against the cage wall, waiting for their eyes to adjust, for their hearts to stop pounding.

"This thing is going to take off soon," Lindy whispered. "We're never going to see home again. Never going to see Mum and Dad. Or our friends. Or anyone." A sob escaped her throat.

Nathan shook his head sadly. "At least we saved Brenda."

"That sick, fat alien had Brenda's head all the way down his throat," Lindy uttered, her face twisting in disgust. Her whole body shuddered. "One more second and. . ."

"And he would have bitten her head off, just like that bird," Nathan said. "If we hadn't begged him. If we hadn't promised to be good slaves. . ." His voice trailed off.

Lindy groaned. "I feel sick. I really do. When he pulled Brenda out, and I saw her head was covered in that yellow slime, like runny egg yolks . . . her hair all sticky and stuck to her head. . ."

"Stop talking about it," Nathan said sharply. "We saved her. She's okay. Now . . . what about us?"

"Yeah," Lindy sighed, holding on to the bars. "What about us?"

"We have to find a way out of here," Nathan whispered. "If the ship takes off, we'll never see home again."

He swept his eyes around the glittery cage. "I . . . I can't even find the door!" he stammered.

Lindy peered out. "All I can see is cage after cage," she wailed. "Little squares piled on top of each other."

Nathan slid his hand along the bars. "Wait!" he cried. "I think I've found the cage door."

He tugged. He pushed. He tried to slide it— one way, then the other.

"I can't move it," he sighed.

"Maybe if we both try to push it," Lindy suggested.

"It's solid metal," he told her. "And it's locked. And I don't see the lock. Or the latch."

Lindy uttered a frightened cry. "We're supposed to be geniuses—aren't we?"

Nathan nodded. "Yes. We know we're superbright."

"So we should be able to think of something."

Nathan peered out through the gleaming bars—and saw Gobbul staring in at him. "We'll be taking off soon," the alien announced. "Try to relax. And don't talk so loud. From the control deck, Morggul and I can hear everything you say."

"Let us go!" Lindy pleaded. "Please!"

"We won't make good slaves!" Nathan cried. "Your emperor will be very unhappy. He'll be very angry. Lindy and I have an attitude problem! A *bad* attitude problem!"

But Gobbul had vanished back to the control deck.

Clinging to the cage bars, Nathan and Lindy both let out unhappy groans.

"Was that our best try?" Nathan sighed. "That was really poor."

"Come on—" Lindy urged. "*Think*. We're geniuses. We should be able to use our brains to escape."

She stared hard at Nathan.

Nathan stared back at her. "Yes. Our brains," he repeated. "That's why they are taking us to their planet, right? Because of our brains?"

Lindy nodded.

They both remained silent for a long while, staring out at the silvery honeycomb in front of them. Then gazing thoughtfully at each other.

"Think. . ." Lindy murmured. "Think of something."

"Wow," Nathan said, shaking his head. "I . . . I can't think of anything. Not a single plan."

"I can't, either," Lindy confessed. "I can't think clearly at all. It's like my brain is on overload or something."

Nathan swallowed hard. Behind his glasses, his eyes grew wide as he turned to Lindy. "The Brain Juice—I think it's wearing off!" he cried.

Nathan grabbed the bars as the cage began to vibrate and rock. He heard a roar beneath him. The whole spaceship rumbled and shook.

"We're taking off!" he cried. "Now what?"

21

"Maybe we can outsmart them when we get there," Lindy said in a trembling voice. "Maybe we can talk to them. Convince them to send us home."

"How?" Nathan asked weakly. He pressed his forehead against the silvery cage bars. "I don't feel clever any more, Lindy. I can't think clearly at all."

"I don't feel clever, either," she confessed. "But maybe it's just because we're frightened. Maybe if we calm down. . ." Her voice trailed off.

"They expect us to be super-bright," Nathan said unhappily. "What will they do to us when they find out we're not?"

Lindy didn't have time to answer.

Morggul bobbed up in front of them. His smooth green skin glistened wetly under the bright lights. "Gobbul and I can hear your lies," he growled. "Our Brain Energizer Fluid is the best in the universe. We know it cannot wear off!"

"But it has!" Nathan started. "Our brains—"

"Silence, slaves!" Morggul ordered. "You cannot fool us." He shoved a stack of papers at them.

Nathan grabbed the papers. "What are these?" he asked the fat alien.

"Puzzles," Morggul replied. "It's a long trip. You need to keep your minds busy."

Nathan stared down at the stack. "Crossword puzzles? How did you know we like these?"

"We watched you carefully," Morggul replied. He held several pencils in one tentacle. He shoved them through the bars at Nathan. "Keep your minds busy," he said. "The emperor wants his slaves to be sharp."

"But—but—" Nathan sputtered.

"You're making a big mistake," Lindy cried. "Turn this ship round. We can't be slaves. You can't do this!"

Morggul didn't reply. He turned and lumbered back to the control deck.

"He—he doesn't believe us," Nathan moaned. "He refuses to believe that the Brain Juice wore off."

"What are we going to do?" Lindy wailed.

Nathan stared down at the first crossword puzzle. He read a clue to Lindy. "Opposite of *go*," he said. "A four-letter word."

Lindy rubbed her chin. "Hmmm..." She thought for a long while. "What is the clue again? I forgot it."

Nathan read it again. "Opposite of *go*. That's a tough one..."

"Let's go on to the next one," Lindy suggested.

"Family pet that purrs," Nathan read. "Three letters."

They both thought in silence.

"Try *dog*," Lindy said finally. "It should fit."

Nathan lowered the pencil to the puzzle and began to write in *dog*. "Do I write in the white squares or the black squares?" he asked.

"The white squares, I think," Lindy replied. "Try the white squares."

"But—the pencil won't write!" he exclaimed.

Lindy narrowed her eyes at him. "You're holding the wrong end," she said. "You're trying to write with the rubber."

"I am?" Nathan stared at the pencil in his hand for a long time. "What's a rubber?" he asked.

They stared wide-eyed at each other. Nathan let the pencils and puzzles fall to the floor.

"We're ... stupid!" he gasped.

Lindy shuddered. A soft cry escaped her lips. "Yes. The Brain Juice wore off. And it's made us stupider."

Nathan shook his head, his expression tight

with fear. "How are we going to escape? We're too stupid to think of anything."

Lindy swallowed hard. "How are we going to *survive*?"

22

They were both sitting on the floor, gazing blankly at the wall, when Gobbul and Morggul appeared at the cage door. "We have landed," Gobbul announced.

Nathan and Lindy shook their heads, as if trying to wake up. "We didn't feel the landing," Lindy murmured. "I didn't hear anything."

"How long was the trip?" Nathan wondered out loud. "I lost track of time."

Lindy stared at her watch. "I think you can tell time with these things," she told Nathan. "But I don't remember how."

Nathan grabbed her wrist and raised the watch to his face. He squinted at it. "Which is the big hand and which is the little hand?"

"We don't have time for this fakery!" Gobbul declared impatiently. "We know how clever you are." He pressed a tentacle against the front of the cage.

Nathan heard a loud click. A buzz. And then the cage door slid open.

The two aliens were breathing hard. The pods up and down their tentacles pulsed and throbbed, opening and closing rapidly.

"I'm so excited," Morggul declared.

"Morggul and I are excited to present you to the emperor," Gobbul told them.

"We're excited too," Nathan replied. He squinted at them. "What's an emperor?"

Lindy scratched her head. "I used to know that word, I think. Give us a hint."

"No more stalling," Gobbul growled. "Come out now. Follow us. We have landed our ship beneath the emperor's palace."

"Beneath?" Nathan asked. "Is that above or below?"

"Be quiet!" Gobbul snapped. "Remember that you are slaves. You will speak only when spoken to."

"But—what will our jobs be?" Nathan demanded shrilly, his voice revealing his panic.

"As the emperor's personal slaves, you will do all of his mathematics for him," Gobbul replied. "You will do all of the difficult calculations. You will—"

"Mathematics? Does that mean *numbers*?" Lindy asked.

"Of course!" Gobbul cried impatiently.

"But we're too stupid to do numbers!" Nathan whispered to his stepsister.

"Ssshhh." She raised a finger to her lips. "Maybe we can fake it."

Morggul turned to Gobbul. "Why are they doing this?"

"They're just frightened," Gobbul replied. "Ignore it. We know how clever they are. The emperor will see."

"Here are your translators," Morggul announced. He slid a silvery chain around each of their necks. "They will allow you to understand our language."

"Hurry," Gobbul ordered. "Follow us. We must take you first to the cleaning room."

"Huh? The cleaning room?" Nathan gasped.

The aliens led them out of the spaceship and then down a long, silvery corridor. Everything appeared to be made of chrome and mirrors. Like the spaceship, everything gleamed and glowed.

Their footsteps echoed loudly as they made their way. Nathan and Lindy had to hurry to keep up with the two aliens.

They stopped at shiny double doors. The doors slid open. They followed the aliens inside a silvery box.

"This lift will take us up to the cleaning room," Gobbul announced. "Remember that you are slaves. You will speak to no one."

The doors slid shut. Nathan felt the pull of the lift as it began to rise rapidly.

"No one will believe their eyes when they catch a glimpse of these two!" Morggul sniggered. "Only two arms. Only one mouth!"

"Yes, they are disgusting to look at," Gobbul sneered. "But they will make excellent slaves."

The lift doors slid open. Nathan and Lindy followed the aliens down an even brighter hallway. The glow from the walls, the smooth, shiny floor, and the mirrored ceiling were so bright Nathan had to shut his eyes.

He felt a chill of fear roll down his body. Panic suddenly froze him. He had to struggle to breathe.

We're on another planet, he thought.

We've been kidnapped.

We're going to be slaves.

The long, shimmering, silver hallway made him feel as if he were walking through a dream. But he knew it was real. The panic that froze his body told him it was real.

The hall opened into a vast area. Nathan gazed up at an immense wall of squares. Like crossword puzzle squares, he thought. Hundreds and hundreds of them covering the walls.

Were they windows? Doors?

Green tentacles wriggled out of many squares. Purple pods on the writhing tentacles opened and closed.

"It looks as if the whole wall is alive!" he whispered to Lindy.

She gazed wide-eyed at the tentacles in the squares. Her mouth hung open. "Why are they doing that? Do they *live* behind those squares?"

A group of green aliens—fat and walruslike—identical to Morggul, lumbered by. They turned and stared in shock at Nathan and Lindy.

"What *are* those?" an alien gasped.

"They are called humans," Gobbul told them, pushing Nathan and Lindy forward.

"Ugh," one of the aliens muttered.

"Faces like a bad dream," another alien sniggered.

"Hurry," Gobbul urged the two frightened kids. "We don't want to keep the emperor waiting."

They passed another wall of squares. Squares from the floor to the high ceiling. Green tentacles twisted and curled out of dozens of squares.

In the distance, Nathan could hear strange music. It sounded like the droning of bees, mixed with the shrill whine of an electric saw cutting through wood.

"Here," Gobbul said sharply. "Here is the cleaning wing. Turn right."

Nathan stopped. He stared from side to side. "Which way is right?" he asked.

Lindy raised her hands and gazed from one

to the other. "One is right and one is left," she murmured. "But how are we supposed to remember which is which?"

"Stop that! Come this way!" Gobbul cried. He shoved them into a large, bright room. Long silvery tables filled the middle of the room. Along the walls, green aliens busily worked at strange electronic equipment. Their tentacles moved rapidly over dials and silvery keyboards.

The walls stretched up for miles. Clumps of aliens walked along a catwalk up close to the mirrored ceiling. The equipment buzzed and whistled. Groups of aliens moved rapidly along the tables, their tentacles curling and uncurling.

Gobbul stepped up to another tall alien with tusks. He said something to the alien in a different language. It sounded like *"Whummp whump whummmp"* to Nathan. The other tusked alien replied with a lengthy *"Whummmmp."*

Gobbul turned back to Nathan and Lindy. "The emperor is waiting to see his new slaves," he told them. "First, we must clean you to make you worthy of being in the emperor's presence."

Two fat, walrus-like aliens pulled long hoses from the wall.

Nathan and Lindy gasped. The hoses were huge, wide as fire hoses. They had big silver nozzles the size of lunch box thermoses on the end.

"Wh-what are you going to do with those?" Nathan stammered.

"We must clean out your insides," Gobbul replied. He motioned to the two aliens. The aliens pulled the hoses closer.

"Open your mouths," Gobbul ordered. "We must do a deep cleaning. The hoses must go all the way down."

Nathan froze in terror. He stared at the big silver nozzles, the huge hoses. "You're going to put those down our throats?"

"It may be a little uncomfortable," Gobbul replied. "But after half an hour or so, you'll get used to it."

"No!" Nathan screamed.

The alien dragged the hose closer. The big nozzle gleamed in the bright light.

"We'll choke!" Nathan cried.

He grabbed Lindy's wrist and spun away.

And before he even realized what he was doing, they were running. Running alongside the silvery tables, down the middle of the room. Past gawking aliens.

"Whump whump whummp!" Alarmed cries rose up around the huge room. Aliens shouted and pointed down from the catwalk on the ceiling.

Nathan glanced back to see Gobbul and Morggul chasing after them.

Pulling Lindy, he burst out of the room. Into the gleaming, mirrored hall. So bright, his eyes watered.

"Where are we going?" Lindy cried in a tiny, breathless voice.

105

"I—I don't know," Nathan gasped. "I can't even see!"

They stumbled forward blindly. Nathan cried out as he ran straight into a wall.

"Ohhh." He felt something wrap round his leg. Some kind of cord? A plant tendril? A snake? And then another one wrapped round his waist.

"Noooo!" He let out a scream. Struggled to free himself.

But they held him prisoner. He turned to see Lindy beside him, held tight against the shining wall. Held there. . .

Held by long green tentacles.

The tentacles stretched out from the squares in the wall. Wrapped around them. Held them prisoner. Purple pods opening and closing rapidly. Hot, sour breath blowing around them.

Gobbul and Morggul stepped up quickly, tentacles waving excitedly in the air. Their four mouths turned down angrily.

"You cannot escape your cleaning, slaves," Gobbul declared. "Where do you think you can run?"

Morggul chuckles. "You can't run home from here!" he exclaimed.

Gobbul turned back to the aliens at the door to the cleaning room. "Prepare the hoses," he ordered. "The deep cleaning will begin—now!"

Two tall, tusked aliens pulled Nathan and

Lindy back into the cleaning room. Two other aliens dragged the hoses over and raised the nozzles to the kids' mouths.

The other aliens stopped their work to watch. Aliens gazed down from the high catwalk. The room grew silent, except for the buzz and whistle of the equipment.

"We ... won't survive," Nathan whispered. "We're doomed."

Lindy let out a choked sob.

The alien pressed the nozzle against Nathan's mouth. "Open wider," Gobbul ordered.

The silvery nozzle felt cold against Nathan's tongue. It filled his mouth. Started to tickle the back of his throat.

"Turn on the cleaning acid!" Gobbul commanded.

24

Acid? Nathan thought.

A cold wave of terror swept over him. His knees buckled. He started to fall.

He heard a rumbling sound. The sound of the hose starting to fill.

Acid?

He shut his eyes.

A voice boomed through the vast room: *"WHERE ARE MY NEW SLAVES?"*

Nathan opened his eyes as the nozzle was pulled from his throat.

"The slaves are being deep-cleaned," Gobbul called, his eyes on a silvery loudspeaker on the wall.

"SKIP THE CLEANING!" the voice boomed, so loud the loudspeaker appeared to shake. *"BRING THEM TO ME—AT ONCE!"*

"We're saved," Lindy whispered.

"For how long?" Nathan whispered back.

*

The emperor's chamber was bathed in a pulsing white light. Brighter than any room the kids had seen.

Nathan cried out and covered his eyes with his arm. He waited for the shock of the pain to fade. Then he slowly uncovered his eyes. Squinting, he struggled to adjust to the blinding, throbbing light.

When he could finally focus, he saw a crowd of green aliens. They jammed the room from front to back. Tall aliens with tusks. Shorter, fat aliens—all glistening with sweat. All murmuring in their strange language, their tentacles pointing excitedly at the two humans.

Nathan huddled close to Lindy, who still blinked painfully in the stunning brightness. Squinting, his eyes swept over the vast room. Over the gleaming mirrored walls. The silvery columns. He gazed up at a domed ceiling miles above. The dome glittered as if covered with diamonds.

And then, Nathan saw the emperor standing in front of a silvery throne.

Nathan recognized him at once. The emperor was taller than the other aliens. He stood very erect, sweat rolling thickly down his emerald body. His tusks were thick and long. At least two feet long, they curled out at the sides like a broad moustache.

Nathan raised his eyes to the crown on the

emperor's head. The crown was the same silvery colour as the tusks. And as the emperor bowed his head, Nathan could see that the crown hadn't been placed on the emperor's head. The crown *grew out of* the emperor's head!

Behind the emperor stood two stern-looking guards. Each carried a long, white, tubelike weapon. They stood at stiff attention, eyes moving over the crowd.

Once again, Nathan gripped Lindy's wrist. His hands were cold and trembling.

Nathan and Lindy hung back as Gobbul and Morggul stepped forward. Gobbul had a pleased grin on both of his mouths.

He bowed low to the emperor. Morggul did a strange, awkward curtsy.

"One and Only, your human slaves," Gobbul announced.

The emperor's eyes bulged as he stared hard at Nathan and Lindy.

They're *all* staring at us, Nathan saw. Hundreds of aliens. Staring at us as if we're some kind of zoo animals.

Or alien slaves.

Nathan shivered.

"Well ... they are not very handsome. Let us see if these humans are smart enough!" The emperor ordered Gobbul, "Prove to us that your Brain Energizer Fluid worked on them."

"It will be my pleasure, One and Only,"

Gobbul replied with another bow. He turned to the two kids. "Move to the wall behind you."

Nathan squinted at him. "Behind us? Which way is that?" he asked.

Lindy shook her head fretfully. "Where do you want us to go?" she asked, looking very puzzled.

"Behind you! Behind you!" Gobbul cried impatiently.

Nathan stepped forward. Lindy turned.

And they bumped heads.

"Ow!" Lindy rubbed her forehead. "Watch where you're going!"

"WHAT IS THE PROBLEM HERE?" the emperor boomed. He grabbed his long tusks with two tentacles. His eyes locked angrily on Gobbul.

"Ha ha. Just a game the humans play," Gobbul explained, forcing a broad smile.

"You claimed you made these humans clever!" the emperor challenged.

"Yes," Gobbul agreed quickly. Beads of thick sweat ran down his body. He was suddenly standing in a puddle of sweat. "They *are* clever. They are brilliant!"

"Brilliant?" Nathan cried. He scratched his head. "Is that some kind of insult?" he asked Lindy.

"Nathan, be quiet!" Lindy scolded. "Don't let them know we're not clever any more."

"WHAT DID YOU SAY?" the emperor

demanded. His voice echoed off the silvery walls.

The room filled with the whispers and excited murmurs of the aliens looking on.

"But I can't help it! I'm stupid!" Nathan protested to Lindy.

"Sshhh. Me too!" Lindy declared. "But we have to pretend—"

"I'm stupider than you!" Nathan declared.

"You are not!" Lindy cried. "I'm *twice* as stupid as you are."

"Twice?" Nathan stared at her. "Is that *more* or *less*?"

"ENOUGH!" the emperor exploded. He raged at Gobbul and Morggul. "Did you think you could *FOOL* me? These humans are morons!"

"No—" Gobbul started to protest.

He didn't utter another sound.

The emperor gave a signal to the two guards. The guards raised the long white tubes.

Nathan saw two bright flashes.

Gobbul and Morggul stood frozen for a moment. Then their heads tilted back. Their tentacles dropped lifelessly to their sides.

Nathan gasped as the two aliens appeared to melt. The green skin melted off their bones. And then their bones crumbled, crumbled to powder.

A second later, there was nothing left.

Nothing. . .

The emperor turned to the guards. He pointed to Nathan and Lindy. "Disintegrate them too," he ordered.

"Noooo!" Nathan let out a terrified cry.

He grabbed Lindy by the shoulders—and shoved her to the floor.

He dropped down beside her.

Two streaks of white light shot over their heads.

Gasping for breath, he scrambled to his feet. His eyes frantically swept the room, searching for a way to escape.

Nowhere to run. . .

If we run into the crowd, we'll be captured instantly.

If we stand here. . .

"Duck!" he shrieked.

Two more white blasts whirred past them. Nathan felt the burning heat from the blasts on his shoulder.

"This way!" Lindy cried. She hurtled towards the emperor, her red hair flying behind her.

Nathan hesitated for a second.

The two guards swung their white tubes round.

Nathan plunged after his sister. They ran right at the startled emperor.

All four of his tentacles flew up above his head. He opened his mouths in a bellow of rage.

Nathan and Lindy dived behind his broad, gleaming throne—as another burst of white light whistled over their heads.

Protected by the throne, they searched the back wall—and saw an open doorway in one corner.

"Can we get to it?" Nathan wondered out loud.

"We have to try," Lindy replied breathlessly.

Nathan took a deep breath and held it. Then, ducking low, running in zigzags, he led the way, running full speed over the shiny mirrored floor.

Angry cries and the thunder of racing footsteps echoed behind them. The whole room seemed to bounce and throb as the emperor and his followers chased after them.

Nathan and Lindy burst through the open doorway together.

Nathan let out a cry and stopped short. Lindy couldn't stop herself and crashed into the wall.

"A cupboard!" Nathan gasped.

They spun round.

"We're trapped!" Lindy sighed. "We ran right into a cupboard!"

"Let's get *out* of here!" Nathan choked out.

Too late.

The emperor filled the doorway. His eyes moved from Nathan to Lindy, and broad smiles—smiles of victory—spread on both of his mouths.

"Let us go!" Lindy cried, her voice cracking.

The emperor tilted back his head and laughed, an ugly, croaking laugh. "Okay," he said. "You may go."

He reached a tentacle up to a silver lever on the wall. He pulled the lever down.

"Nooooo!" Nathan uttered a terrified howl as the floor slid away beneath him.

Nothing to grab hold of. . .

No floor . . . no floor. . .

He felt himself falling. "Ow!" He landed hard on his back and started to slide.

He and Lindy were both sliding, side by side. Screaming as they fell.

Sliding down through darkness, faster. Faster. . .

A horrifying ride to their doom.

26

"Nooooooooo!" Their shrill screams echoed through the darkness.

Suddenly, light poured over them. Nathan saw a hatch open below them.

They slid through the hatch. Landed hard, in a sitting position on a mirrored floor.

Bars slid around them. A door slammed shut.

A prison cell? A cage?

His heart pounding, his throat sore from screaming, Nathan squinted into the white light. Slowly, his eyes began to focus.

"Where are we?" Lindy asked in a whisper. "Are we dead?"

Nathan shook himself as if trying to force away the terrifying feeling of falling. He struggled to clear his head.

He heard a rumbling beneath them. The silvery bars began to vibrate. The floor shook.

He turned to Lindy. "We're back on a spaceship," he said. "We're taking off."

Lindy swallowed hard. When she turned to Nathan, her eyes brimmed with tears. "Do you think they're sending us home?" she asked. "Do you think we could be that lucky?"

Two days later, they were at Uncle Frank's house, desperately trying to describe what had happened to them. Both talking at once, talking without taking a breath.

"Whoa. Slow down. Slow down," Dr King pleaded. He scratched his red cheek. "One at a time, okay?"

He hugged them both for the twentieth time. "I'm just so glad you're okay. Jenny and I took the first flight back from Sweden. We were so worried when you disappeared."

"We never thought we'd see home again!" Lindy cried.

"But they didn't want us," Nathan explained. "We weren't smart enough. So they rejected us. They sent us back."

Uncle Frank narrowed his eyes at them. "First you became amazingly smart," he said. "Then the juice wore off?"

"Yes," Nathan and Lindy replied in unison.

"We became stupider and stupider," Nathan said. "And then, as soon as we returned home, we became normal again."

Uncle Frank clapped his hands together. "Wow. This is an *amazing* story!" he exclaimed.

"We must call the newspapers. We must call the TV news! We have to—"

"No!" Nathan and Lindy insisted. "No way!"

He squinted at them. "What are you saying?"

"We just want to be normal!" Nathan declared. "We don't want to be freaks. We don't want people staring at us. Not believing us. Giving us a hard time because we're different."

"Nathan is right," Lindy said. "We want our friends back. And we want to go back to our school. We want our normal lives back. We don't want to tell anybody about being kidnapped by aliens."

Uncle Frank rubbed his chin thoughtfully. "Okay, okay." He sighed. "I understand."

He glanced at the blackboard on the wall. It was covered with numbers. An endless equation.

"Now that I know you two are okay, maybe I can get back to work on this impossible equation," he said, shaking his head.

They heard the kettle begin to whistle in the kitchen. "Sit down, kids," Dr King said. "I'll be right back with that hot chocolate I promised." He hurried from the room.

Nathan wandered over to the blackboard. He picked up a piece of chalk. He studied the long equation for a moment.

Then he began furiously writing numbers and

letters. "There," he said, after a few seconds' work. "I solved it."

"Nathan!" Lindy gasped. "Rub it out! Hurry!" She ran up beside him and shoved the eraser into his hand. "Hurry! No one is supposed to know—remember? Everyone has to think we're normal now."

"I know. I know," Nathan groaned. He began to rub out his solution to the equation. "I can't help it," he whispered. "It's almost impossible not to use my brain. Back on that weird planet, it was *so hard* to pretend to be stupid!"

"Well, it got us home—didn't it?" Lindy replied. "It was a brilliant plan. But from now on, we have to be very careful. If we want normal lives, we can't let anyone know we're the smartest people on earth!"

Nathan rubbed out the last numbers just as Uncle Frank returned to the room, carrying a tray with their drinks on it. "Here you go," he said. He handed Nathan and Lindy steaming white mugs of hot chocolate.

"What's that *you're* drinking?" Nathan asked, pointing to the tall glass in Uncle Frank's hand.

"This?" Uncle Frank held up the glass and grinned at Nathan and Lindy. "It's grape juice. Same brand I gave you. I've been drinking it eight times a day. Can't hurt—right?"

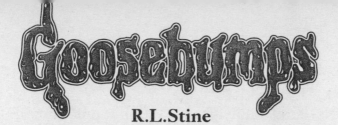

Goosebumps

R.L.Stine

Reader beware, you're in for a scare!

These terrifying tales will send shivers up your spine:

Reader beware – you choose the scare!

Give Yourself Goosebumps

A scary new series from R.L. Stine – where *you* decide what happens!

Choose from over 20 scary endings!

GOOSEBUMPS

Reader beware — here's THREE TIMES the scare!

Look out for these bumper GOOSEBUMPS editions. With three spine-tingling stories by R.L. Stine in each book, get ready for three times the thrill … three times the scare … three times the GOOSEBUMPS!